www.ChloeEmile.com

Molly's Story

Brides of Fall River

CHLOE EMILE

This is a work of fiction. Names, characters, organizations,places, events, and incidents are either products of the author's imagination or are used fictitiously.

Molly's Story
Copyright © 2015 by Chloe Emile. All rights reserved.

ISBN-13: 978-1987859201
ISBN-10: 1987859200

Contents

CHAPTER ONE

1871, America

Braxton Calhan worked for his father's law firm in New York. He was unquestionably a fine lawyer, but he also enjoyed long lunch breaks, especially on warm summer days.

On one of those lunch hours, he passed by an author's reading of his new novel in the park and happened to notice a young woman sitting on one of the benches. Braxton didn't care about the author nor the book; he only had interest in the young woman. With long brown hair, porcelain skin, and dark eyes, she was stunning.

He stood there for over half an hour, sneaking glances at her, then slowly made his way toward her once the lecture was over.

As she got up, she dropped the book from her lap. Braxton saw his chance, and he gracefully bent down to pick it up and hand it back to her, smiling at her.

"Thank you." She smiled back politely.

"You're welcome," he replied. "Did you enjoy the book?"

"Yes, very much, didn't you?"

He understood he was supposed to give his opinion about the book. Braxton decided to do the only thing any man in his position could do: he lied. "Well, truthfully, I feel there were a few chapters that seemed to repeat themselves."

To his relief, the young lady smiled. "That's how I feel, especially the last two chapters."

You're one lucky man to pull that one off, Braxton thought to himself. "Can I walk you somewhere?" he asked.

"Well, I'm heading to the station. I should be heading home."

"Oh, do you live somewhere in the city?"

"Not really."

He looked at her closely. She was really beautiful, and he feared he would never see her again once they got to the station. He had to think of something and fast.

"Do you come to the city often, Miss..."

"I come down when there is a good lecture. It is quite a train trip to get here. And my name is Molly, Molly Lochlan, Mr..."

"Calhan, Braxton Calhan. My friends call me Brax."

When she smiled, Braxton noticed she had the slightest hint of a dimple on her left cheek.

"He was a good speaker, too, wasn't he?" Molly remarked.

"Who?" Brax asked.

Molly laughed. "The novelist."

"Oh, right. He wasn't a bad speaker for a writer. They're usually quiet and introspective, aren't they?"

"Maybe," Molly said, smiling.

She talked about more of the novel's plot. Braxton picked up that it seemed to be some sort of saga about a family on a farm. He chimed in that he enjoyed the romance of the main characters, as she did.

They turned the corner, and the station was right there. Braxton scrambled his brain once more for some way to keep in touch with the lovely young woman.

"Miss Lochlan, may I ask you, where do you live?"

"Fall River," she answered.

"Fall River," he repeated, so he wouldn't forget.

"Yes. It's not far from Boston, you know, in Massachusetts."

"Maybe I'll visit there someday."

"Well, this is where we part, Mr. Calhan. My train is on the other side. Thank you for walking me to the station. Maybe we'll run into each other again sometime in the park."

She extended her hand, and Brax shook it.

"It was truly a pleasure, Molly. I do hope we meet again."

She turned and headed for the platform to wait for her train. Braxton had no choice but to return to his office. He had taken two hours for lunch on his one-hour lunch break. Still, he took his time walking back to the office, feeling happy and glum at the same time—happy he'd met Molly but glum that she'd left an instant later.

On the train ride home, Molly looked down at the book on her lap. She knew Braxton had not really read the book. The last two chapters were not repetitive at all. She'd known he was lying, but she'd let him keep on talking.

She didn't know why. Maybe she found him amusing, or maybe she just found him handsome. He was tall and broad shouldered, with dark hair and eyes. *Just the way I like them.*

Whatever the reason, he did intrigue her. Even if she never saw him again, she would cherish her short afternoon with him in New York. After all, he did have a nice smile, and he had gone out of his way to impress her.

She looked out the window as the train pulled away from the platform. When she closed her eyes, she could still see his smile. *You're being silly, Molly. He can't be interested anymore. Not when they are so many beautiful women in New York City. Why would he be interested in a farm gal?*

At twenty-one years old, she didn't feel like a woman yet. *What would a man from the city want with a girl from the country?*

Braxton Calhan sat at his desk, staring blankly out the window, thinking about a little town called Fall River and a young lady named Molly Lochlan.

For some reason, he couldn't get her out of his mind. She wasn't like any of the girls he knew. Braxton was constantly surrounded by society-bred women who liked to flock to all the young men at every social affair. They'd all gone to the finest finishing schools, yet didn't have the sense to come in out of the rain, as his mother always said.

How could a chance meeting for such a short time stay so strongly in his mind? He was a twenty-six-year-old, successful New York attorney clinging to the memory of mere minutes he'd spent with a young lady he would probably never see again.

He had to find a way to get to Fall River. Braxton was so lost in his thoughts of Molly, he didn't hear his father come into the office.

"Brax?"

Braxton jerked his head toward the door and saw his father.

"Sorry, Dad. I didn't hear you come in."

Carter Calhan looked at his son. "You seem to be a bit preoccupied this afternoon," he said, " as though your thoughts are a hundred miles away. What's her name?"

Brax blinked at his father. "Her?"

Carter smiled. "Yes, 'her.' You have a moon-struck look in your eyes, and you're smiling and looking out the window when there's nothing to see. It can only be because of a girl. I'm willing to bet that if the building was on fire, you wouldn't even smell the smoke. Am I right?"

"But how did you..."

"You have the same look I had thirty-eight years ago. I was walking into the bank, and I saw the most beautiful young woman. Brax, when I tell you she was beautiful, that's an understatement."

Braxton was surprised. His father's life revolved around work, and rarely did he talk about his feelings.

"Did you talk to her?" Brax asked.

"Of course I did. But she was only visiting from Virginia. It was her first time in New York, and, well, the city was a bit overwhelming. She asked me directions to some bookstore, which I'd never heard of, but luckily, I knew the street. I gave her directions and then turned around and went to work. Once I was back in the office, I couldn't stop talking about her. She had morning-blue eyes and hair the color of corn silk." Carter smiled at his son wistfully. "So I know that look well. It's obvious it's because of a girl."

"Whatever happened?" Brax asked. "Did you ever see that girl again?"

"I should say so." Carter chuckled. "I married her, and she's still the same beautiful woman I met thirty-eight years ago."

Brax looked at his father in surprise. "Mom? You never told us this story."

"Well, maybe I didn't feel I needed to tell you and your sisters, but when I saw you with that look on your face, it brought back some memories."

"I doubt I'll ever see her again," Brax said. "She only comes down for lectures."

"Lectures?"

"Yes. She reads all those literary books—the ones I could never really get interested in or understand."

"Hmm. Seems like she's got a head on her shoulders and she's not just another pretty face." Carter shook his head at his son. "Oh, you'll see her again; don't worry about that. I have a feeling that you'll make it happen. These kinds of meetings are once in a lifetime."

A week went by, and still Braxton couldn't break from the spell of Molly Lochlan. Her smile haunted him, and the way the light danced on her hair would wander in his thoughts. His work hadn't suffered, but he'd spent most of his nights staring at the ceiling in his bedroom, unable to sleep.

He finally realized the only thing to do was to find her somewhere in Fall River, Massachusetts. With his mind made up, he set off for the little farming town.

CHAPTER TWO

At the Fall River train station, a train pulled in, and only one passenger got off: a smartly dressed young man carrying a small overnight bag. Art McClain, the station manager, came out to offer his services to the tall stranger, who seemed to be looking a little bit lost.

"Can I help you?"

"Yes, I'm looking for the Lochlan home."

"Oh, you must be here for the wedding. People have been coming since yesterday. If you'd like some advice, you best get a room at the hotel before they're all gone."

Brax heard nothing after "the wedding." His heart filled with dread. "Wedding?"

"You mean you're not here for the wedding?" Art asked.

His mind raced. *Wedding? Whose wedding? Have I missed my chance and Molly is getting married?*

"If you like, I can get you a horse to get out to the Lochlan place," Art said.

"A horse? You mean to ride? I never ride. We don't ride in New York."

Art figured the man needed a carriage. "I can go to the livery and see if Ray Teal is up. He can take you."

"If you can show me where the livery is, I'll go myself," Braxton said.

"Just down the street. It's the last building on the left. You can't miss it."

Brax picked up his bag and hurried down the street without looking back. He wondered if he had made a mistake coming.

It couldn't have been Molly's wedding. She would have said something when they'd met. Getting married wasn't something a lady would omit in conversation with a fella who was clearly interested. But then again, she really hadn't said much, and people don't just tell total strangers that they're getting married.

As he got to the livery, Brax noticed a faint glow through the window. He knocked on the door lightly. When he got no response, he knocked harder. Then he heard footsteps.

"Hold your horses. I'm a-coming," a voice said from inside.

The door opened slowly, revealing an old man's friendly face.

"Hello, Mr. Teal. I was told you could supply me with a carriage?"

"I could," the old man said jovially. "Come on in. It'll take me a minute to get the horses hitched up. Going to the wedding?"

"How did you know?"

"Well, I figured. After all, folks have been coming in all day, folks that ain't ever been here before, and the only thing going on is the Lochlan wedding."

"I had no idea she was getting married."

"No idea? Shoot, she's been engaged to the Bradford boy for a year. Fine young fella she met in Washington last year, when she went to visit her aunt and uncle. Everyone said it was love at first sight. After we saw them together, we knew it was only a matter of time. I tell you, those Lochlan girls, all three of them, each one is pretty as a picture. It won't be long before the other two get married."

"All *three*?"

"Why sure," Mr. Teal said. "The girls are triplets. Meghan, Molly, and Annie. You telling me you didn't know?"

"No, I didn't." Braxton sighed with relief. "So it's not Molly who's getting married?"

The old man smiled at him. "Shoot, heck no. Miss Molly's not even close to getting married. Not saying she ain't had any fellas looking her way, her being so pretty and all. There's been many young fellas lookin' her way, thinkin' about askin' her to a dance or something, but, well, Molly doesn't seem interested in anyone yet. From the way you been askin' questions, I'm thinkin' you are a bit sweet on Molly. Well, I can't blame you. She loves her critters, and they love her. She's the one who is most like her mama, Miss Abby. The woman is an angel walking on this earth. Why, there ain't a livin' soul who doesn't love her."

Braxton started to relax. Perhaps he still had a chance with Molly.

"You take my word, young fella, if you really are interested in Molly, you'd better like critters—and that means horses. She's very fond of horses. She's especially fond of her Shamrock, a fine horse, fast as the wind."

"Well, I..." Brax was embarrassed that his interest in Molly was so transparent to everyone.

The old man gave him another knowing smile. "I'll get the team hitched up for ya. Make yourself at home."

Brax sat in the chair on the small porch and waited. He let out another sigh of relief and closed his eyes until Mr. Teal came out of the stable with the carriage ready.

"Here ya go, young fella. Now if you follow the road for about two miles and then come to a fork in road, take the road to the right, and that will lead you right to the house."

"Thank you."

As relieved as Braxton felt, he still had to figure out how to explain to Molly what he was doing there, at a wedding of a bride and groom he didn't even know.

"Hope you enjoy yourself," the old man said.

"I'm sure I will," Brax said, but he didn't feel as confident as he sounded.

He got on the carriage, took the reins, and started to move down the road.

At the Lochlan home, Annie was helping with the final touches on the bridesmaids' dresses. Of all the girls, Annie was the best at sewing. She had a natural talent for it and even helped Mrs. Whitlock, the dressmaker in town, whenever she needed help getting an outfit done.

Molly was the second born of the Lochlan triplets. Older sister Meghan had come into the world fifteen minutes earlier, and younger sister Annie had been born twenty minutes later, with a little help from their grandfather.

Each girl was different in every way, yet they were bonded by family and faith. The Lochlan home was filled with loved ones for the upcoming wedding on Saturday. All the guests had already arrived, and the five bedrooms were not enough, though.

Molly had not forgotten the handsome young man. He seemed to have a stronger hold on her than she'd thought. Every time she looked at a book, any book, it reminded her of him. With all the family preparing for her sister Meghan's wedding, Molly felt it was best not to bring up her last visit to New York. A girl's wedding was an important day, and Meghan deserved to have all the attention.

With so many people moving about, it was a wonder that anyone noticed Braxton driving up the road toward the house. By chance, Mick had looked out the window and noticed a young man looking completely out of place.

He mentioned it to Ryan Lochlan, Molly's father, and both men went out to talk to the stranger in the carriage.

"Can I help you?" Mick asked.

He took a good look at the young man's face and instantly recognized him. Mick had seen him a few years back in New York at a function with his father that they attended for the state department. Braxton probably didn't remember him, but he and his father had certainly left an impression on Mick.

Carter Calhan had a reputation for being demanding with his employees and his clients. He was intense, the kind of man who liked to get his way, though his kind son seemed nothing like him.

"Yes," Braxton replied. "I'm looking for a Miss Molly Lochlan."

"You're Carter Calhan's son, aren't you?" Mick asked.

"Yes, sir. I'm Braxton Calhan." Surprised to be recognized, Brax stuck out his hand to shake Mick's.

"Mick Dawson," he said, shaking Braxton's hand. "I met you and your dad a few years ago at a function."

Braxton had heard of Mick. He was a well-respected name in Washington and was reputed to be fair and honest.

"Yes, your name sounds familiar, Mr. Dawson. I've heard a lot about you."

"Well, don't hold that against me."

As Braxton came down from the carriage, Mick turned to Ryan.

"This is Braxton Calhan. He is with a very fine firm in New York called Calhan, Stamford, Willis, and Finner. Mr. Calhan, this is Ryan Lochlan, Molly's father."

The smile on Braxton's face turned serious as he shook Ryan's hand.

"So you know my Molly, do you?" Ryan asked sternly.

Ryan and Mick felt this was a good time to have some fun with this young lad. The men both looked at Braxton with suspicious eyes, giving Braxton a very uneasy feeling.

"I can assure you it was a very proper meeting, and all I did was to walk her to the train station."

Ryan cocked his head at him. "How did you know she lived here? You must have asked her."

"Well, yes, I did ask her. I mean, it came up as we were walking to the station. I assure you it was all very innocent."

By that time, Abby had come to the front of the house. She saw the men at it again. They were drilling a poor young man, and Abby knew she had to save him. "Hello, I'm Abby Lochlan. I don't believe I've had the pleasure."

Her smile and pleasant voice immediately put Braxton back at ease.

"I'm pleased to meet you, Mrs. Lochlan. I'm Braxton Calhan, from New York."

As hospitable as always, Abby put her arm in his and smiled again.

"Well then, Mr. Calhan, do come with me around back and have something to eat. You will be staying for supper, and I won't take no for an answer."

She turned and shot a look at Ryan and Mick. "You gentlemen can join us if you like," she said sharply.

And as soon as Abby and Brax were out of the others' earshot, Abby laughed and said, "I think I came just at the right time to get you away from them."

"Yes, ma'am." Braxton let out an uneasy laugh.

Mick and Ryan looked at each other and shook their heads.

"She's done it again, Mick," Ryan said.

"Always cutting into our fun," Mick agreed.

Abby turned to Braxton. "Tell me, Mr. Calhan, have you come for my daughter Meghan's wedding or to see my daughter Molly?"

Once again, Braxton was surprised by how transparent his motives were. "How did you..."

"Oh, it's easy, Mr. Calhan. I asked Meghan's fiancé if he knew who you were. He didn't. And you told me you're from New York. Molly was just in New York, so it's safe to assume you're here for her. Am I right?"

"You're very good, Mrs. Lochlan. Have you ever thought of going into law?"

"Not really. By the way, just call me Abby. Everyone does."

"Well, Abby, yes, I met Molly in New York. This may sound crazy, but I can't get her out of my mind. You think I'm crazy, don't you?"

"Not at all. As a matter of fact, I think it sounds very romantic. Like a romance novel. I love those, don't you?"

"I'm afraid I don't read many novels," Braxton admitted.

"On second thought, it's probably not the type of book a man would read. My Ryan certainly doesn't."

Once they were in the back of the house, Abby introduced Braxton to the guests.

"Everyone, this is Braxton Calhan, a friend of Molly's."

Molly stood up. She was indeed shocked at the sight of the young man in her house. She associated him with New York. She quickly worried if she looked all right. Was her hair in place? Was her dress flattering? Did she look too pale? She pushed aside her surprise and doubts, and walked over to him with all the confidence she could muster.

"Well, hello. I must say I didn't expect you to come up so soon."

"Well, things were slow in New York, and... and I had to come to this magical place called Fall River."

"Magical place?"

"You see, I heard that there's a beautiful princess who is only allowed to leave this magical place once a month and the last time she met this young man, they spent only a short time together, and, well, when she left, she took a piece of his heart with her."

"Oh, have you come to take it back?" Molly smiled.

Just then, Meghan came over to him, after making the rounds to talk to the guests before she got ready for the ceremony.

"I'm Molly's sister, Meghan. My, you are a handsome one. It's a shame I'm getting married."

Braxton felt himself getting a bit embarrassed, his cheeks flushing lightly. He finally was able to get out a shy thank you before another fine young lady approached him.

"Don't pay her no mind," said the lady, who looked remarkably like Molly. "I'm Annie, and I say you are welcomed here."

Annie, like her mother, managed to make matters comfortable.

Mick came over to him. "Are these girls bothering you?" he joked. "Sorry about earlier, son. We were just having some fun with you."

"What do you mean?" Molly asked Mick. "Were you and Daddy bothering Braxton?"

"Now, why would I do a thing like that, Molly girl?" Mick said innocently. "We were just talking to the lad. Isn't that right?"

Braxton only looked at Mick. "You're Molly's uncle?"

"You didn't tell him?" Molly asked Mick.

"No, he didn't," Brax said.

Mick smiled. "Truth be known, Molly darlin', it never did come up."

"Uncle Mick, I can't believe you and Daddy both." She turned back to Braxton. "I'm sorry about these two. They did the same thing to Adam, Meghan's fiancé, when he first came to visit. Uncle Mick, you both promised Mama you wouldn't do it again. Oh, wait till I tell her."

"Now, Molly darlin', you wouldn't tell on your dear ol' uncle Mick, would ya? After all, you know how your mama gets when she gets mad. She's not one to get riled up." He turned to Braxton. "She's a lovely woman, but when she's riled up—well, let's just say hell hath no fury like my sister-in-law when she's mad."

For the rest of the evening, Mick and Ryan were on their best behavior. Brax enjoyed Molly's tactic to keep them in line. Too bad she wasn't an attorney; she would have made a good one.

When everyone was distracted, she did manage to walk off with Braxton down the road and away from the crowd.

Finally, Brax could tell her everything he wanted to. He tried to sort it all out in his head. It had sounded so good when he was thinking about it on the train. But the words just wouldn't come out.

"So you never said what brought you here, Mr. Calhan. Although I like your story of the magical place, I need more than that. Are you thinking of changing your profession to write fiction?"

Braxton smiled. "If you must know, it was you. Ever since I met you that day in the park, I can't seem to get you off my mind. Now, don't go looking at me like you think I've lost my mind. I haven't, and I wanted to get that all out in the open. Was it too much for me to come here?"

"You came to see me? I must admit that I didn't expect to see you here. I'm touched, but a bit confused. I mean, I have never had anyone travel all these miles just to see me."

Her response surprised him.

He hadn't expected her to rush into his arms, but he at least thought she would be happier than that. Instead, she'd sounded cool and indifferent.

They continued to walk toward the stables, and he remembered that Mr. Teal had said she loved critters, especially her horses. She walked ahead of him into the stable, where she went straight to a beautiful chestnut with a white blaze.

"Do you like horses, Brax?"

"Well, living in the city, one really doesn't have much use for one," he said truthfully.

"True, but that was not the question I asked you."

"Well, no, I'm sorry. I don't like horses, to tell you the truth. I'm afraid of them."

Molly gave the horse her attention. She took a brush and began combing the horse's mane. A few minutes passed, and Brax only stood by, a good distance from the horse.

"Well, it seems I was mistaken," Brax finally said. "I thought you would be happy to see me. I thought we had felt there was something special we shared. I see I was wrong. Maybe I was a fool to come here. It seems you prefer to be with your horse. I'll save us both the embarrassment of me staying longer and will leave now. Don't worry, I know my way out. You can stay with your horse. Goodbye, Miss Lochlan."

With that, he left her in the stable and headed back to the house to get his carriage. Ryan saw him as he was getting back into his carriage.

"You leaving so soon, Mr. Calhan? It sure can't be because of Mick and me. We was only foolin' with ya, son."

"No, it seems I've made a mistake. Your daughter was not pleased with my arriving here. Do give my apologies to Mrs. Lochlan. If you'll excuse me, I want to get back to town and get the earliest train back to New York."

He took the reins and made his way down the road toward town. Molly came back to the house just as Braxton drove past her. She raised her hand, yet he just kept looking forward as if she weren't there.

"Trouble, Molly girl?" her father asked her.

"Oh, Daddy, seems I messed up everything."

He put his arms around her, and she began to cry.

"Now, Molly, it can't be all that bad."

"I'm afraid I scared him off. I tried to be more like Meghan. You know, I just acted like I didn't care. It always worked for her. Well, it backfired. He said he had made a mistake coming here, and now he's gone. He told me he came here just for me. Daddy, no one has ever done something like that just for me. Oh, Daddy, I really made it worse."

"Well, he couldn't be much of a man to let you scare him off. I mean, I don't think I like any man who makes my girl cry. Doesn't seem like a gentlemanly thing to do."

"Oh, but he is, Daddy. He's smart, and he's kind and wonderful and..."

Ryan looked down and smiled at her. One look in her eyes told Ryan all he needed to know.

"And you really like him, don't you, lass?"

She nodded, and tears filled her eyes again. He hugged her tightly and tried to find something to say to make her feel better, but he just didn't know what to say. At times like that, he felt useless because he couldn't take the tears away and make it all better.

But maybe he could. There were no trains until the morning. Perhaps he and Mick could pay Brax a little visit later.

CHAPTER THREE

Brax arrived at the livery and knocked on the door. Mr. Teal took longer to open up than he had before, and the waiting tried Braxton's patience. When the old man finally came to the door, his kind smile disarmed Braxton.

"Well, young fella, you lost the way to the Lochlan house?"

"No, I was there. I'm returning your carriage and heading to the train station to get the first train back to New York."

"Something wrong?" Mr. Teal frowned, causing all the wrinkles on his forehead to show up.

"Yeah, I should have stayed back in New York."

"Now why would you want to say something like that?"

"She didn't care if I was there or not. All she wanted to know was if I liked horses."

"There's your first mistake. Seems you're only half listenin' to the gal when she's talkin' to ya. Didn't I tell ya she had a special feelin' for horses? Look, I know those girls, and if Molly spent more than a polite few minutes with you, she likes you. Did you tell her you like horses?"

"No, I told her the truth. I'm afraid of them."

"Oh, lad, that was not the time to be truthful. Come inside. You can't get a train till morning anyway, and I have some fresh coffee on the stove."

Braxton followed the old man inside. He was impressed by how neat and clean Mr. Teal kept the little kitchen. Mr. Teal went to the cupboard and took another cup from the shelf.

"Make yourself at home, fella. By the way, what is your name?"

"Braxton Calhan."

"Calhan? You any kin to Carter Calhan?"

"He's my father."

"Well, this is a small world. I knew your daddy when he was about the same age as you. Me and the missus had a small inn in some small town in Virginia. Your daddy had come a-riding up to the place. One could see he was bone tired, and the poor horse was not much better; if he went another mile, he would've been dead. I put the horse in the stable for the night and rubbed him down. I told the young fella to go inside and rest. My missus felt sorry for him and gave him a hot meal and a chance to sit by the fire. He told us he was trying to find a young lady he had met in New York."

"That is quite the coincidence." Brax shook his head in disbelief. "It *is* a small world."

"Seems she was visiting friends in New York when they met. She must have left some kind of impression, 'cause he came all the way here to find her. I can remember my missus sat up with him most of the night as he told her about the young girl. My missus, she had a soft spot for others in trouble. And she felt this young fella needed someone to hear his story just to listen, nothing else. When he left the next day, we hoped he would find her. Say, did he ever find her?"

"Yes." A proud smile played on Braxton's lips. "She's my mother. Funny, my father told me the story a few days ago. That's what made me come here."

The old man nodded. "Oh, I would have loved my missus to know that. He found his young girl and I have a feeling you will, too, lad. Don't give up. I tell you, son, I know Molly, and she wouldn't lead you on. The girl doesn't have a mean bone in her body. Not anyone in the family does. Her grandfather was a fine man. He raised those three girls on his own after his wife and little girl were killed."

"Killed?"

"Something about the rights to the road and the railroad. I wasn't here at the time. As I heard, it was the railroad and Abby's dad that had the dispute. Something about money that Daniel never got for the railroad to use the road. The road is a private road owned by Daniel, and seems the railroad wanted to use it, since it was a short route to the railroad camp down by the river where their crew was laying down track. That's when Ryan stepped in. Seems he worked out a deal between the railroad and Daniel. All seemed to be fine until the day that Daniel and the family were going off to a picnic and a shot rang out just as they got to the main road. The first shot killed Molly, his wife, and the second killed the little girl, Annie. They never did find out who shot them, as far as I know."

"Molly's named after her grandmother, I take it."

"Yes," Mr. Teal said, pouring Brax a cup of tea. "Abby named her. Her sister Annie died, and unfortunately, so did her other sister Jenny. Jenny was married to Mick, but after they divorced, she was killed in a train accident. Have you met Mick?"

"Yes. He seems like a nice man."

"A few years ago, Mick married Abby's other sister, Mary. They moved to Washington."

"That's quite the story," Braxton said.

Mr. Teal nodded. "An interesting family. Miss Abby, she's a stubborn one. She loves that ol' farm just like her ma and pa and refuses to leave for anything. All of Abby's girls take after her in different ways. They're fine girls."

Brax thought about that train in the morning. Did he really want to go back to New York so soon?

Mr. Teal seemed to be reading his mind as he drank from his cup.

"Well, sonny, have you made up yer mind?"

"Sir?"

"Is ya gonna stay or head back home? Mind you, though, if ya do leave, you may never get the chance of knowing if lightnin' strikes twice."

Braxton gave him a confused look.

"If it worked for your pa," Mr. Teal explained, "don't you think it will work for you?"

Brax recalled the happy look on his father's face when he'd told him he had married the girl he went to search for. His father never thought of anything but work, so it had been unusual to see him gush over something else for a change.

"You're right, Mr. Teal. I'm not going back, not just yet anyway. I figure Molly Lochlan is worth another try."

The old man put down his tea. "That's what I wanted to hear. You know, sonny, I have a feeling that our Molly has met her match. I'd like to see her married off, and you seem to be the right enough guy to be the one."

CHAPTER FOUR

Meghan looked breathtaking in her gown, and the bridesmaids were equally beautiful in their light-blue dresses, Meghan's favorite color. Father Cahill and most of the guests had arrived.

Upstairs in the girls' room, Annie was putting the finishing touches on Meghan's veil. Each girl would carry a single red rose, and Meghan, the traditional banquet. Downstairs, Mick and Ryan helped Adam get ready. However, Mick, as usual, was not helping.

"So, Adam, now you tell me you plan to live part of the time in Washington and the other part in Pennsylvania. That doesn't leave any time to come home to Fall River for a visit. I'd hate to think that my niece won't be seeing her family as often as she should."

"Well, can the family come to see us?"

Adam looked to Ryan for help, but he only shrugged.

"Come to visit you?" Mick started again. "And who do you think will take care of the farm while they are gone? I tell you, lad, I have never had the pleasure of them coming to my home in Washington, though the girls have been there a few times. Oh, yes, that's how you met Meghan."

"Well, maybe we can figure out some arrangement out to make a few visits," Adam said.

"I'd be thinking on that, laddie. I sure wouldn't want to think that you'd be keeping my Meghan from seeing her family."

Mary, Mick's wife, came down the stairs and saw Mick and Ryan's playful expressions. She knew right away that they were teasing the poor groom. She walked toward them, intending to interfere, but she heard a knock on the door.

Mary answered, smiling at the stranger. "Can I help you?" she asked the handsome young man.

"Yes, I would like to see Molly. I know it's her sister's wedding day and all, but it's important." He sounded so sincere and looked so vulnerable.

"Do come in. I'll get Molly for you. Do have a seat, Mr..."

"Calhan, ma'am, Braxton Calhan."

"Yes. Well, do sit down, Mr. Calhan."

Mary went to look for Molly. On the way, she threw looks at Mick and Ryan, imploring them to behave.

"Hey, there's the guy who walked out on our Molly last night," Mick said. "I thought he was heading back to New York."

"Well, let's see what he has to say for himself," Ryan said.

They walk over to Brax, who was in the seat by the door.

Mick pretended to be surprised. "Well, look here, Ryan. It's our ol' friend Braxton. I thought you said he was going back to New York."

"That's what Molly told me," Ryan said, ignoring Brax. "Seems they had a slight disagreement, and he left her in tears."

"Tears, you say? He left our Molly in tears. Fancy that, and he's back here again. Could it be he's going to break her heart again? I do hope that's not on his mind."

Braxton's eyes widened as he looked back at the men and shook his hands. "That's not how it was at all, sir. If you'll let me explain—"

"Really," Mick said. "Are you calling my niece a liar?"

"Sir, I'm telling you it was not like that," Brax protested.

"Suppose you tell us what really happened."

"She asked why I showed up, and I told her I'd come because I wanted to see her. She didn't seem to care. I figured I didn't mean anything to her at all, and I left in a hurry. I must be crazy to think that she cared, but I came back today to see one last time. If she tells me to go, I'll never bother her again. You have my word on that."

As if on cue, Molly came down the stairs. When she saw Brax, her cheeks flushed, and she almost ran back up. Instead, she took a deep breath then slowly made her way toward him.

"Molly, dear," her father said, "you have a guest. Now come down here and make him feel welcomed."

As she got closer, Brax stood up, and she smiled at him. Brax thought she looked lovely in her light-blue dress. It complemented her dark hair and eyes well.

"Mr. Calhan, you came back."

"Yes, I did..."

Music sounded, and Molly looked out the window.

"The wedding is about to start. If you care to wait, I'll speak with you after the wedding. This is Meghan's day, and we'd like to give her the spotlight, so to speak."

"I will wait only so long, Molly Lochlan. If you're not interested, I will leave and never darken your door again. But I promised myself one more try."

Molly nodded. He was serious. And so was she. "I promise, I'll talk to you after the wedding, Mr. Calhan."

She went to leave, then he touched her arm.

"Braxton or Brax. My father is Mr. Calhan."

"Very well, Braxton."

CHAPTER FIVE

Meghan was absolutely radiant in her white dress, a truly beautiful bride, yet Braxton never took his eyes off Molly. The thought of talking to her again made him anxious. She was still acting cool, but if Mr. Teal was right, the fact that she'd asked him to stay was a good sign.

Abby noticed that the young man's gaze was solely on Molly from the moment Molly stepped from the back door. Molly never once glanced his way, yet her daughter probably knew that Brax was sitting the back row, his eyes fixed on her. Abby smiled. Her daughter's own romance was just beginning. *Fitting that it would begin at a wedding*, she thought.

True to her word, at the end of the ceremony, Molly made her way back to Braxton.

"Shall we go somewhere that's a bit less crowded?" she asked him gently. "I promise I won't take you to the stables. But one day, I will cure you of your fear of horses." She looked out the window, and Brax stood up to look with her. "Past that tree is a nice spot. I used to go there to sort my thoughts when I was younger."

He held out his arm, and she placed her arm in his as they walked up toward the mound of trees. The feeling of his arm in hers felt so right, as if it had always belonged there. She was so glad he'd come back; she had been certain that she had lost her chance when he left.

"So what did you want to talk about?" she asked.

"Molly, I'm only going to say this once. I came here to Fall River to see you. I can't seem to think of anything else but you. I know you think it sounds crazy, but truth of the matter is, up until last month, I had no idea that's what happened to my father also. He met this girl from Virginia in New York, and he went to Virginia to find her, just like I did to find you."

"Did her find her?"

"He did. She's my mother!"

He noticed the surprise on her face.

"Now I'm not saying we are like them, but I would like to know you better, Molly. If you don't think it's possible, I'll just leave and never bother you again."

He stopped and waited for her to answer.

A moment of silence passed, then Molly finally looked up at him. "I would like very much to get to know you better, also, Mr. Calhan."

They both beamed at each other.

"You would?" Brax said. "You really would? I was hoping you would say that. I really didn't want to walk away from you."

She shook her head. "I was so upset when you left. I thought I messed everything up and that you'd gone back to New York. I thought I would never see you again. I felt I would have to go to New York and hope you would be in the park again. I had such silly ideas. How would I know you would be at the park again?"

He looked deep into her dark eyes. "You can't shake me that easily, Molly Lochlan. I'm a stubborn man, full of pride. I like to win, especially when it's something I really want."

She laughed. "Oh, really? I'm also stubborn, and I usually get what I go after."

"So this is how it's going to be, is it? Winner takes all?"

"I wouldn't have it any other way, Mr. Calhan."

"And the winner gets what, Miss Lochlan?"

"Marriage!"

Only after she'd said it did she realize her boldness. It was too late—she couldn't take it back, and she didn't want to.

Brax stepped back to examine her to see if she was serious, then he broke out into a bigger smile. Before she had time to change her mind, Brax agreed to it.

"I accept the prize of marriage to you. I look forward to winning this."

Thus was the beginning of the strangest courtship that anyone had ever heard of.

CHAPTER SIX

They saw each other once a month, and most of their time was spent on the train to New York and back.

Molly still read her books, usually on the train. She had managed to cure Braxton's fear of horses by teaching him to ride. It'd been a bit awkward at first, and she'd had to admit he was really bad at the beginning, but she knew she needed to have patience with the boy. After all, he was born and raised in a city, where there wasn't much use for riding horses.

Braxton found everything about her new and exciting. When he'd first seen her in the park, she'd looked like a model in a storefront window that had come to life before his eyes, and yet in Fall River, she was a totally different woman. He found it hard to wrap his head around.

On one of his visits to her hometown, they were walking toward the lake when he saw a deer walk up to her and eat berries out of her hand.

"Did you just feed that wild animal?" he exclaimed.

"White Tail? She's no wild animal. She's been around here for almost two years now. She's very gentle. Would you like to feed her?"

"No." Brax stepped back. "I'll take your word for it."

Suddenly, a raccoon jumped out from behind a tree and ran up to Molly. She cooed down at the animal.

"Well, hello, sweet one. How are you this afternoon?" She dug into their picnic basket and took out some apple slices, which she offered to the raccoon.

"I suppose this one is tame also?" Brax asked.

"Don't be silly, Brax. They are not tame, but they're not afraid of me, either. They know I would never harm them, just like that wolf behind you."

"Wolf!" Brax exclaimed. He jerked back to look for the wolf and scared the animal back into the woods.

"Now look what you've done. You scared him."

"Scared *him*! Molly, this is not normal. How can you expect anyone to sit calmly with wild animals coming down and walking up to you!"

She only smiled and shook her head. "This is who I am, Brax. I'm not some dainty little lady who never gets her hands dirty. I love my critters and will always be the one who takes in a stray and nurses it until it's healthy enough to go back out into the wild again."

As if on cue, a falcon landed near Molly.

"This here is Fly Boy. He had a problem with his wing a few years back. Well, with Doc's and my help, he was ready to join his friends again, and he stops by here now and then." She looked at the bird with affection. "Don't ya, Fly Boy?"

Brax only looked at her incredulously.

Later that evening, at the supper table, Abby asked if Brax had enjoyed his walk in forest. Molly watched him, waiting for how he really felt.

Always the frank one, Brax said, "Well, it was an experience, I must say."

"How so?" Abby asked.

"I mean no disrespect, Abby, but your daughter is..." He stopped when he realized all eyes were on him. He had to choose his next words carefully.

"You were saying my daughter is what, Brax?" Ryan asked.

Brax gulped. "Well, her thing with animals—it's just not like a girl to, to..."

"To what, Brax?" Abby asked gently. "Is there something wrong with her treatment of animals?"

"Oh no, not in the least. Ma'am, she's got names for all of them. Do you know she has a wolf cub?"

Abby smiled. "Oh, you mean Gray Eyes. He's been coming around here since he was a pup. Hunters killed his ma. Molly bottle-fed him till he was able to be on his own. He's as tame as a puppy."

"Ma'am, in Boston and New York, folks don't have animals like that as pets."

Molly stepped in. "Brax, I told you they aren't pets. They're just friends."

"That's just it. Normal folk don't have wolves at their house."

Ryan and Abby looked at each other. They knew their daughter well enough to know that was the wrong thing to say to Molly. She got up from the table.

"Well, maybe it's a good thing we found this out now, about what *normal* people do. If you all will excuse me, I'm going to sit outside so the normal people won't be offended by me." She left the dining room in a huff.

Brax sat there in shock. He looked to Ryan for help, but his eyes did not look friendly. Then he looked to Abby, imploring her to understand his words. Ryan stood and walked after his daughter.

As Annie prepared to clear off the table, Abby turned to Brax. "Perhaps we should go into the living room."

As Abby started to get up, Brax quickly went to her to pull out her chair. Abby smiled, knowing that the little things Brax did made him seem odd in her daughter's eyes, just as Molly's love for critters made her odd in his.

When they had settled in the living room, Abby tried to explain about Molly.

"Let's see, where do I begin? Molly is a very special girl. But you know that already. When she was very young, she had this way with animals, all animals. Why, Ryan put her on a horse when she was three; it was so natural, it was like she was born on the saddle. She's what folks say is a natural with animals. You take Shamrock out in the stable—Molly raised him from a colt, and there isn't any horse around that can match his speed. She's won as many ribbons in racing as any man this side of Boston."

"But Abby, it's dangerous—"

"Brax, Molly is what she is. She knows how to be a lady, but she also knows that with her family and friends she can just be Molly. You should feel lucky she let you in that private world only the very few can see."

Meanwhile, on the porch, Ryan was trying to explain to Molly why Braxton didn't understand her fondness for animals.

"You see, Molly girl, some men—not all, mind you—just don't seem to understand how a female can have this natural talent with animals. Oh, I've seen it before. Why, back in Ireland, most of the womenfolk in my home town had this ability with animals. My mother included. Why it got so when a cow was having a calf, they'd call my mother instead of the veterinarian."

He laughed as she looked at him doubtfully.

"You're making this up, Daddy."

"I sure am not. I'll have you know, we always had fresh milk and butter on our table every day, thanks to your grandma. She was a great woman. You remind me of her with your way with critters."

"Do I really?"

"Yes, you do. Oh, I wish my dear parents could have been alive to see what fine grand-children they have. You all would have made them proud. I know it would please them because you all have made me proud."

Molly leaned over and gave him a hug. "I love you, Daddy. You always know what to say."

"I love you, too, lass."

Brax came out on the porch, and Ryan stood up.

"I'll give you two some privacy."

When Ryan closed the door behind him, Brax sat down and took Molly's hand.

"I'm sorry if I offended you. You see, I didn't grow up with a lot of animals. You know I'm scared of them. I'm not used to them and think they're dangerous. I suppose I got a little worried about you."

Molly smiled and squeezed his hands. "Okay. I understand. Just as long you don't think I'm a wild animal myself."

"I don't. You're like an earth goddess. I may not completely understand why you want to spend so much time with wild animals, but if it makes you happy, don't mind me."

"Thank you, Braxton. I appreciate it. Animals are lovely creatures. I hope you get over your fears one day."

"With you to guide me, I'm sure I will."

CHAPTER SEVEN

After the third month of being with Molly, Brax invited her to the Calhan home for an informal party. The guests included partners in the law firm as well as their wives.

The Calhans had a lovely Fifth Avenue apartment with a beautiful view of the city, especially at night. Brax and Molly arrived early in the evening, and as Brax helped her out of the carriage, Molly was a bit taken aback by how tall the building was. She began to have doubts about being at the party.

Sensing her nervousness, Brax asked, "Is something wrong?"

Molly played with her handkerchief. "I don't know all these people. I don't think... I just don't fit in here. I'm just a..."

"You're just perfect. Molly, do you think I care what they think? I'm not giving up; I want to win that prize, remember? I want you to be my wife."

She squeezed his arm in gratitude, and they walked up the front steps to the door.

The doorman opened the door for them with a pleasant smile. "Good evening, Mr. Braxton."

"Good evening, Cecil. Cecil, this is Miss Lochlan."

He tipped his hat to her and smiled.

"It's a pleasure to meet you, Cecil."

"The pleasure is mine, Miss."

"Just call me Molly. Everyone does."

The young couple walked into the lobby. Braxton led her to a door, and when he opened it, Molly thought it was odd that the inside was the size of a closet, not another room, as she expected.

A gentleman in a uniform stood inside the closet.

"Hello, Mr. Braxton."

"Hello, Charles. Charles, this is Miss Lochlan, and she's never had a ride in an elevator."

"Well then, we must give her the full treatment." Charles tipped his hat to her. Miss, you just need to step in here along with Mr. Braxton. Once the door is closed, you will feel a movement. That's to be expected. The room is going up to the floors above us. It's really nothing to be upset about, and, well, you'll see."

Within moments, Molly did feel the "room" moving. "Oh my, Brax, it really is going up."

Braxton smiled. What he took for granted was all new to Molly. When it reached the floor where Brax's parents lived, the "room" came to a stop. Charles opened the door, and Molly realized they were on the top floor. She hesitated in getting out.

"Go ahead, Miss Lochlan. It's safe to step on the floor."

Braxton stepped out first then reached for Molly's hand. She stepped out, too, relieved to have made it.

"It has been an honor to give you your first ride, Miss Lochlan," Charles said.

"Thank you, Charles, and you can call me Molly."

They walked down the hall toward the sounds of laughter. Suddenly, Molly's feet froze to the floor. She simply couldn't move another step.

Braxton looked back. "What's the matter?"

"I'm sorry, Brax. I just can't. I don't belong here. I just want to go back home."

"Molly, you will do no such thing. You said you never give up. Well, if you do, this would mean you would lose."

She went over to one of the chairs against the wall and sat down. "I can't do it. Braxton, I can't change who I am. Please don't make me go in there. I don't belong in that world."

Just then, the door opened, and Susanne Calhan came out. She saw Molly in the chair and recognized the nerves in the poor girl. She closed the door, shutting in the music and laughter, and gently walked over to Molly. "My dear, can I get you something? Perhaps some water?"

"No, ma'am, I'll be fine. Maybe if I could just go back to the station and..."

Susanne sat down on the chair beside her. "Why, you'll do no such thing. Go through the back, and you can relax in the guest room. Braxton, take her to the side door and to the bedroom to the far right."

Molly looked up at her with startled eyes. "No, you don't understand. I really would rather..."

"You'd rather run—I know. I was that way myself when I first had to face these old windbags. I wasn't like them at all. Heck, with all those fancy forks on the table, I had no idea which one to use. Why, back at home, we had only one fork, and we were lucky to have that."

A small smile started to spread on Molly's lips.

"Believe me, when I first came to one of these parties, I really was so scared."

"What did you do to make it better?"

"I got to thinking that they weren't too much different than me. I watched and listened to what they were talking about and kinda felt my way in slowly."

"Oh, I don't think I can do that."

"Just follow me, and I'll show you all the shortcuts."

Molly took a deep breath. "Okay."

"You've got the confidence in you," Susanne said. "Come on; let's go through the front door."

"I'm really not that confident."

"If you're not, you can pretend. No one would be the wiser." Susanne got up and offered her hand to Molly. "Get ready to walk in the front door, Molly. Let's go and knock 'em dead."

Braxton opened the door for them. "Come on, Molly. You are a beautiful girl. Let's make the world see just how beautiful you are."

Susanne and Molly walked in, arm in arm.

"Ladies and gentleman, may I present to you Miss Molly Lochlan."

All eyes turned to Molly, and she blushed but kept a confident smile on her face, just as Susanne had instructed. The guests seemed to be looking back at her with pleasant expressions.

Carter Calhan was the first to walk over to them. "You know, we were all thinking Braxton was just fooling us about how pretty you were," Carter said. "Well, now I can say that he really does have it right. You would be a hard young lady to get out of any man's mind. Permit me to introduce myself. I'm Carter Calhan, Braxton's father."

Molly smiled. "Thank you for your kind words, and it is a pleasure to meet you, Mr. Calhan."

"Now, Carter," Susanne said, "you and Braxton entertain the guests. I want to chat with Molly."

She put her arm around Molly's shoulder, and they headed off through a long hallway.

Once in a private room, Susanne closed the door. "Well, see. It wasn't so bad, was it?"

Molly shook her head. Susanne gestured for her to sit down on a dark-green couch, and she did.

"Good. I want to tell you a story about a young girl a lot like you. She came to New York after running away from home. Oh, she wanted to have a new life, a different one. Well, this handsome man met her on a main street. She pretended she was lost and needed directions. He was very nice, and it wasn't long before they were having lunch. He took her to the train station and watched as she boarded the train back to Virginia. Now that was not the end of the story. Not more than three weeks passed before that same young man found the young girl in her hometown, and before the day was over, they were married."

"Have you ever regretted any of it?" Molly asked.

"Regret? No. We have three beautiful children, four grandchildren, and I've just met the woman who just might very well be my son's wife."

Molly's eyes widened. She looked down at her lap.

"Don't look so shocked, dear. I've seen the way Braxton looks at you, and I'm so glad he's found someone who is perfect for him."

"But I'm so different from the city girls."

"So was I, dear. I'm still myself, and I only made a few adjustments to fit in. Besides, I have a husband who accepted me, and that's all I ever needed. Now, are you ready to go out there and face those old biddies? Don't forget, I'm right there if you are in doubt. Just ask me if you need any help."

They headed out to the party just as the butler announced that dinner was served.

Braxton went over to Molly as his father took his wife's arm to walk to the dining room with the other guests. Susanne had arranged the seating so Molly was sitting right beside her. Molly was thankful Susanne had placed her that close.

"Tell me, Molly," Carter said, "Braxton says your family has lived in Fall River for years. They were there before the railroad came."

"Yes, that's true, Mr. Calhan. My father and Uncle Mick had come down from Boston to work on the railroad. That's how my father met my mother."

"Father, I believe you know her Uncle Mick," Braxton said. "Mick Dawson. He works for the state department."

"Yes, I met with him a few years ago, back here in New York. So Mick is your uncle?"

"Yes, he's married to my aunt Mary, who is my mother's sister."

Around them, the guests at the table were all talking, and that gave Molly a chance to observe what went on in the so-called informal parties. The men usually talked of business, and the women smiled politely and complimented each other on what they were wearing. They gossiped about frivolous things. Molly realized she could not, and would not, be one of those women.

While they were waiting for dessert, she caught Braxton's eye and looked at the balcony. Braxton caught the hint. "If you gentlemen will excuse me, I think I'd like to show Molly the sights of New York from the balcony."

"Is it only the sights you want to show her, Brax?" one of the men joked.

Brax took Molly's arm and led her to the balcony.

"Thanks for rescuing me," she said.

"Well, Mother and I had it worked out that one of us would keep an eye on you all night."

The evening was clear, and the view from the balcony was truly awesome. Molly stepped closer to the edge.

"It's beautiful." She surveyed the lights of the building. *Imagine, all these people squished together in one place*, she thought. Fall River had nothing but open space.

Brax put his arms around her waist. "Do you think you could live here, Molly? Could you give up all you have back home and be here?"

She turned her head to look him in the eye. "I don't know, Brax. I really don't know. This is all so new and exciting, but I'm not sure I'm ready for it all, not just yet, but maybe one day."

He held her closer to him. "At least it's not a no."

"Oh, Brax, I'm sorry. I can't give you the answer you want. It's all so new and..."

"I understand, Molly. Tell you the truth, after seeing your world, I don't think I could leave it for this, no matter how tempting it seems. New York is a fast place. People never sleep. I'm only exaggerating, but you know what I mean. But remember this, Molly, I love you and will wait for you to find a compromise. If it takes forever, I will wait for you. I thought I'd be able to walk away, but I just can't. It's like you have me under a spell, and I never want to break away."

"I don't want you to walk away. I believe in you, and maybe I just want it all. Is that so much to want? Is it too greedy of me?"

He looked deep into her eyes and knew he could not refuse anything of her. He gently kissed her cheek. "You are truly the love of my life," he said. "I don't care what anyone says or thinks. I have found you, and I'm never letting you go."

Susanne looked out toward the balcony and saw Brax and Molly in each other's arms. She backed into the hall so as not to disturb them. She liked Molly and was glad Braxton was serious about her.

Later that evening, after the guests had gone for the night, Susanne sat with Carter in his study. "I find the young Lochlan girl charming. I do hope we made a good impression on her. What do you think, Carter?"

Her husband was distracted with papers on his desk. She sighed, not surprised in the slightest. "Carter! Have you heard anything I said?"

He looked up at her. "I'm sorry, dear. I was just looking over some briefs that Stamford was going to resend to the judge tomorrow. I wanted to make sure they were in order."

"Do you possibly think you could forget about that blasted law firm for one night and listen to me? This is our son's future we're talking about. Not your latest merger with some bank."

He put the papers in the desk drawer and looked up at his wife. "All right, Susanne, I'm listening."

"I was just saying I hope we made a good impression on Molly."

"Of course we did. The girl is perfect for Braxton. She's young, and with a little coaching, she will be a valuable asset to the firm. Not to mention she has a very nice inheritance. I heard about her family background, seems the grandfather had set all his girls up very nicely and their children, also. Seems Brax has stumbled upon a wealthy young lady."

"Carter Braxton Calhan, will you stop looking at people for what they can do for you and your blasted firm. You did this to Janie's and Barbara's husbands, and you will not do this to Molly. Don't you understand Braxton doesn't care if she has money? He cares about *her*."

"Your daughters didn't listen to me and married below their station. Look where it got them. One living in some town in Nevada, following her husband's dream that will never come true. The other one married to an army officer, living wherever he's sent to."

"You had no right to force the girls to follow your rules. Janie's husband wanted to own a store, yet it wasn't good enough for you. You had planned her to be married to your partner's son, but clearly neither was interested in the other. Then you tried again with Barbara, but she was too smart for you."

"She wasn't that smart. Look at the life she has now, moving from post to post, never setting down roots."

"Carter, do you realize that you have grandchildren that you have never seen? Don't you want to see and know them?"

"They are not my grandchildren. I have no daughters."

Susanne sighed again. "If you force Molly to change, she will leave, and that will destroy Braxton. Do you want to lose the only child you have left? After losing your own daughters, I didn't think you would do it again. I will not let you do this."

He turned to his wife. "Don't you tell me what to do, Susanne. Braxton will do as I ask, and he will not question me."

"Are you really sure about this one, Carter? Just remember, Molly Lochlan has grit, and she will stand up to you, and if and when she does, you'll lose Braxton. Because if she walks, so will Braxton. You've lost control over him. How does it feel to be alone?"

CHAPTER EIGHT

Susanne left her husband in the study and went down the hall. Halfway down, she decided to stop and head across the hall to the guest room where Molly was staying. She tapped gently on the door.

"Molly, it's Mrs. Calhan. Are you asleep?"

"No."

"I'd like to come in and talk to you."

Susanne heard the footsteps, then the door gently opened. Molly's pale face peeked out.

"If you're not sleepy," Susanne said, "I'd like to talk to you."

"Of course."

Molly let her in. She sat on the bed as Susanne took the chair across from her.

"Did you enjoy the party?" Susanne asked.

"It was very nice," Molly replied. "I'm sorry if I didn't say much, but it was my first party in New York. I didn't want to do anything to embarrass you or Braxton."

"Don't be silly. You were wonderful. I hate to tell you, my first party was a total disaster. My mother-in-law was not a nice woman. She had wanted her son to marry someone of class and wealth, but Carter, well, he'd had other ideas. Anyway, she was determined she would see me fail at the first party and Carter would wake up to his senses. The maid was a sweetheart and she helped me and taught me the right fork to use and even how to hold the knife. That night I pulled it off and my mother-in-law was fit to be tied."

"But why did she dislike you so?" Molly asked.

"I suppose she felt that Carter could have done better. That he should have married one of the many young debutantes here in New York."

Molly's complexion turned even whiter.

"Don't think I feel that way," Susanne said. "I haven't seen Braxton this happy in years. I totally approve of you. I hope my husband doesn't scare you off."

"Oh, I don't scare that easy, Mrs. Calhan."

Susanne smiled at her. "I didn't think you did, Molly. You're going to do just fine in this family. Carter has been toying with the idea of opening a branch office in Boston and having Braxton run it. I think he can if he's got the right woman beside him. What do you think, Molly?"

"Does Braxton know about it?"

"He knows there has been talk, but he doesn't know if it's definite yet."

"Then why are you telling me this?"

"Because I told my husband to offer it to Braxton with the condition he should butt out and let him run it his way."

"I see."

"I don't think you do. I know my son. He can run the firm, but he can't do it with his father breathing down his neck. But with you beside Braxton, Carter will have no control. That was my suggestion to him. If you love Braxton, join him in this. If not, don't hurt him by giving him false hope."

Molly nodded seriously. "You have my promise, Mrs. Calhan. I will never hurt Brax."

Three months later, Molly felt it was time to give her answer to Braxton. She agreed to become his wife. The wedding was set for the fall. The Lochlan girls loved the colors of fall. The Calhans sent out announcements and placed a formal announcement in the newspaper.

Mr. and Mrs. Ryan Lochlan of Fall River Massachusetts announce the engagement of their daughter Molly to Braxton Carter Calhan esq. son of Carter and Susanne Calhan of New York. The couple will be married at the Lochlan farm, and a gala reception is to be held in New York the next day. The couple plan to live in Boston, where the groom will open a law practice.

Back in Fall River, the engagement announcement was made in church after Sunday service. The families had planned engagement parties in Fall River and New York to accommodate the many friends on both sides.

With so many details and seating arrangements, Molly was so thankful to her mother and her sister Annie for helping out. Meghan had sent a wire, stating she would be there the week of the wedding—Adam was tied up in Washington and couldn't possibly be there before then.

Susanne Calhan wrote to say that she and Carter would be attending the wedding and the in-law luncheon three weeks before the wedding. This would give the families a chance to meet and plan the reception at the farm and the reception in New York.

Looking at the RSVP, Molly had her misgivings. It must've showed on her face, because Abby asked, "Is something wrong?"

"Oh, Mother, Braxton's family is coming for the family supper."

"Well, that's wonderful. I'd like to meet Mrs. Calhan."

"Oh, you'll like her. She's lovely. It's Mr. Calhan that I'm worried about."

"Why is that?"

"Mr. Calhan is used to getting his own way. He feels having Braxton move up to Boston would give him some freedom, when he wants the control."

"Oh, don't be silly. Braxton is a grown man and will run his own business."

That afternoon, Braxton arrived at Fall River. He had stopped in Boston earlier and purchased the office building his father had picked out; Carter wanted everything ready for Braxton to move in right after he came back from his honeymoon.

Ryan met Braxton at the train station.

"Did you have a good trip, Braxton?" Ryan asked.

"As good as can be expected, sir. How have you been?"

"Fine, just fine."

Brax got into the carriage, and they headed toward the farm. Brax had always enjoyed the ride out to the farm. Something was peaceful and calm about the land, and he understood why Molly loved it so. With nature and colors all around, the scenery was definitely a big change from the gray hues of the city.

"I envy you," Brax said to Ryan. "You have all this. I can understand what Molly loves about it."

"It's true; Molly and all my children love this land. Sure, they all learned to work the farm, but my son Daniel takes care of most of the farm these days. Tom is still trying to find his place in this world."

"You seem to give your children freedom," Brax remarked. "Your sons, and your daughters of course, are lucky. That's what makes you different than my father."

"Oh, lad, I'm sure your father is a fine man."

"Trust me, sir," Brax said. "My father has only one thing on his mind, and that is maintaining his stellar image. That's where you two are completely different. That was not an insult, sir," Brax quickly added. "I meant it as a compliment. I've seen you with your children, and you always put them first, making them see they can achieve their goals, always encouraging them. My father, well, he makes you strive to be better, but, well, he'll always take the credit."

"Sounds like you're a bit hard on your father," Ryan said.

"I really wish I had a father more like you," Brax said.

"Well, lad, when you marry my Molly, I will be your father if that makes you happy."

Brax smiled at him. "It would make me very happy, sir."

"And you are to stop calling me *sir*."

The carriage turned in the road and slowly made its way up the private road toward the house. On the front porch, Abby was sitting by the roses. She smiled and waved when she saw the men. She got up and walked toward the front door, which was slightly open, and called for Molly.

"Molly, Braxton is here," Ryan called as he came down from the carriage.

Abby came down the front steps to greet him first. "It's so good to see you again."

She always made Brax feel completely at ease. From the first time he had met her, he'd known she was a true caring soul. He jumped down from the carriage and gave her a hug.

"It's good to see you, too, Abby."

Molly came out the door. "I see I've caught you again with another woman in your arms," she joked.

"I confess you are right, but you can't blame me. She's such a beautiful woman and the mother of another beautiful woman." Brax smiled and gave Molly a hug. "How's my favorite girl?"

"Fine now that you're here." Brax looked back at Ryan. "I don't know how you stand it, sir. Being surrounded by all these beautiful women all the time."

"Oh, I manage to bear the burden," Ryan said. "Sometimes, it seems so hard, but I make it through."

Abby gave him a gentle poke to his ribs. "So I'm a burden to you, am I?"

"One that I welcome each day and one I will welcome and thank the good Lord for every day of my life."

Annie came out. "Hi, Brax."

"Hi, Annie," Brax said. "Is your sister keeping you busy?"

"Is she ever! But now that you're here, maybe she won't have so much time to give me work to do."

Brax gave Annie a hug, too. "I promise I'll keep her busy for at least two days. Will that be enough time for you?"

"Thank you." Annie gave a look of mock relief.

"Tell me, Braxton," Ryan said, "where can you drive up to a home and be greeted by three—count them—three beautiful ladies all at once?"

Braxton looked at Ryan then back at the ladies on the porch.

"Nowhere at all. Only in this magical land called Fall River."

CHAPTER NINE

The day finally arrived when both sets of parents were planning to meet to finalize the wedding plans. Braxton and his parents arrived late in the afternoon because Carter had last-minute documents he needed to sign and have completed before the judge. As they got off the train, the argument Susanne Calhan had started in New York was still happening.

"The one day I ask you to take a small caseload so we can arrive before everyone sits down to eat, and you decide you had to take a full caseload. Honestly, Carter, sometimes I feel we're just around as ornaments to you. Your real love is the firm."

Brax interrupted. "Mother, I know you're upset, but can we end this until we get on the train again to go back home?"

Susanne sighed. "Of course. At least I can be civil, even if your father can't."

"I'll get the carriage at the livery," Brax said. "If you wait here, I'll be right back."

Brax took off down the street to Teal's livery, glad to be away from the parental bickering, if only temporarily.

The old man was outside the stable door. "Hey, young fella, how are you? Need a carriage?"

"Yes, I do, Mr. Teal. I also have some people I want you to meet. Would you come up to the train station with me?"

"Well, sonny, I'm not really dressed to meet anyone. Could we make it another time?"

"It's really important, Mr. Teal."

"Well, if it's that important to you, sure I'll come up."

The two made their way up the street.

As they approached, Carter recognized the old man. He ran up to him. "Ray, Ray Teal!"

The old man blinked at Carter, then recognized him, too. He broke out into a wide grin.

"Carter, well bless my soul. It's been too many years, boy."

"That it has, Ray. Tell me, is the missus around? I'd love to see her."

The old man's eyes got moist. "No, son, she passed on about four years ago."

Brax saw that even his father had a tear in his eye when he heard that.

"She was a lovely lady," Carter said. "I would be lost if it wasn't for her that night. She sat up and listened to me. I have so much to thank her for. I wouldn't have my son, and I wouldn't be who I am."

Both men bowed their heads, remembering the lady they'd both loved.

"Ray." Carter looked up. "I want you to meet the gal I went looking for."

"Your boy tells me you found her. How I wish the missus was here. She would have loved to meet her."

They went to the platform where Susanne was standing.

"Susanne," Carter called. "I would like you to meet the man who helped me find you some years ago."

Susanne looked at the old man approaching and immediately recognized a kind soul. She offered him her hand. "May I say thank you. I know it's been a long time coming to you, but thank you so much."

Ray blushed. "Shucks, ma'am, it wasn't all that much. It was my missus who sat up with him all night, listenin' about this pretty girl who stole his heart back in New York and how he had to find her."

"Well, then I must thank her. Is she around?"

Carter looked at her and shook his head. "I just found out she passed on."

Susanne looked at Ray, and her heart went out to him. He was such a sweet soul; she had to do something for him. She had an over-whelming urge to hug him.

"Mr. Teal, you're coming with us to the Lochlan farm."

"Ma'am?"

"I won't take no for an answer."

"Ma'am, I'm not dressed, and I really..."

Susanne turned to her son. "Get the carriage and help Mr. Teal get ready. He's joining us for supper."

The men knew they wouldn't hear anything different, so Brax followed Ray back to the livery.

"So that's the gal Carter traveled to Virginia for," Mr. Teal said.

"Yep," Brax said, smiling.

"Well, I must say she's a fine-looking lady, and I think the missus would approve. She kinda had a soft spot for your pa, and I know she would have taken to you also."

Meanwhile, back on the platform, Susanne looked at her husband with softer eyes. "So that's Ray Teal. You only mentioned him once in all the years I've been married to you. It's funny. For a moment, I saw the Carter Calhan I fell in love with and married. That sweet old man brought back someone I had lost somewhere along the way. I hope I can find him again."

Unfortunately, Carter wasn't listening. He was probably off in his own world, thinking of the money he was either losing or could have been making if he were back in New York. The man she'd seen a few moments ago was lost again.

Moments later, Ray and Brax rode up the street in the carriage and stopped right at the end of the platform. Brax got down and offered to help his mother up.

"Thank you, Braxton." She took his hand.

Ray looked very presentable in his shirt and jacket.

"Why, Mr. Teal, you look absolutely handsome."

"Now, ma'am, I wouldn't go that far, but I do thank you for the compliment."

Before long, they were on the road leading to the Lochlan farm. Braxton looked worried.

"I hope we're not too late," he said.

"Nonsense," Carter said. "No one eats before seven thirty or eight o'clock."

Susanne looked at her husband. "This was supposed to be a luncheon, not a dinner. And this is a working farm. These people get up before the sun does—something you haven't done in years, except when you party all night and come home drunk."

"I have never heard of someone meeting future in-laws over lunch."

"How would you know?" Susanne retorted. "You never bothered to meet your daughters' in-laws at all."

As the carriage drew near the house, Braxton saw Abby and Ryan on the porch.

"They're Molly's parents," Braxton said.

Abby smiled and waved, and Susanne returned the gesture.

"She's lovely," Susanne said. "I can see where Molly gets her looks from. They are a handsome couple."

Ray agreed. "Three girls, triplets, and not an ugly one in the bunch."

"Triplets?" Susanne exclaimed. "That's something you don't hear every day."

"And they have twin boys also."

"Well, that's a big family!"

Ray pulled the carriage to the front steps and stopped. Abby was the first to come up to the carriage and greet them in her usual warm manner.

"Welcome to our home." She looked over at Ray and smiled. "It's so nice to see you, and you're looking very dapper."

Susanne explained. "I invited Mr. Teal since he is an old friend of my husband's and they just reunited here. I hope you don't mind."

"Of course not. Ray is always welcome here. He knows this. Don't you, Ray?"

"Yes, ma'am. Thank you, Miss Abby."

Brax helped his mother down then officially introduced his parents.

"Abby, Ryan, these are my parents, Carter and Susanne."

"Hello." Ryan shook their hands.

"So glad to finally meet you," Abby said. "We just love Braxton, and he's told me so much about you. You're from Virginia; am I correct?" she asked Susanne.

"Yes, from a little town," Susanne said. "My parents were farmers and had a ranch, not as elegant as yours, but it was home to us."

"Oh, when we were growing up," Abby said, "it wasn't as big as it is now. My sisters and I were in one small bedroom, and my parents had the other. We only put the extension on after the triplets were born. We needed more room, and then two years later, the twins came."

"You had your hands full; I can see that."

Brax was pleased that his mother and Abby were getting along so well.

"Look at me standing out here," Abby said. "You must be tired after the long train ride. Do come in to freshen up."

"Oh, thank you," Susanne said. "I would like that."

The women headed inside, leaving the men outside. Carter stood there, looking around the grounds.

"It's a nice little place you have here, Lochlan," Carter remarked.

"We think so."

"My son tells me you've been here for over twenty years. So I take it you know the people well."

Ryan didn't know what he was getting at, but Brax, who did, decided to change the subject.

"Well, what do you say we all go in and relax before supper?" Braxton said.

Carter looked at his son. "Boy, I am talking to Mr. Lochlan. If you want to go inside, go right ahead."

Ryan saw a bit of what Brax had been talking about earlier. "To tell you the truth, Mr. Calhan, I would like to go inside. I don't discuss my business outside. It's a superstition of mine." He turned to Ray on the carriage. "Come inside, or do I have to send Abby out to get ya?"

"No, no, I'm coming, Ryan." Mr. Teal jumped down.

The four men went into the house.

CHAPTER TEN

The dinner was more than informal. Carter Calhan never kept the conversation focused on the wedding, and he was more concerned about the neighbors and area attorneys. It got so bad that Susanne had to stop him.

At the end of the main course, she stood up. "I'm sorry. I must apologize to all of you. You have been so gracious to have us in your home. I am truly touched by your kindness. My husband can't seem to drop the business end of his life at the office and enjoy this dinner with all of you. The numerous questions he's asking you is because his firm is opening a branch in Boston, and he plans to have Braxton run it. He wants to know if they can count on enough clients to keep it going. I felt this would be a good time for all of us to get to know each other and become a family, but the only thing he's interested in is turning this into a business meeting. If you'll excuse me, I think I'd like to go outside for a while." She abruptly walked out of the dining room and out the door.

Everyone turned to Carter, who mustered a grim forced smile.

"My wife doesn't understand about how competitive business is. I apologize for her rudeness."

Abby looked at him. "Mr. Calhan, I didn't feel she was rude or wrong in her comment. This is not the time or place to discuss business. This was a luncheon to discuss plans for the wedding of our children, which for you was not important. I find it hard to believe you are Braxton's father. Your son is warm, compassionate, and has a heart. If you'll excuse me, I will join Mrs. Calhan on the porch."

With that, Abby got up and left the room. A shocked Carter looked wide-eyed at Ryan, Mick, the girls, and lastly, Brax.

Abby Lochlan had just told off Carter Calhan—in front of not only his son but the entire Lochlan family, as well. Braxton savored every moment.

Outside on the porch, Susanne apologized to Abby.

"I'm sorry for my behavior. It's inexcusable. I just don't know what came over me."

"I saw nothing wrong, Susanne. I was ready to say something if you didn't."

Susanne let out a small laugh. "I suppose you and your family will think differently about us after this."

"Not really, but I want to tell you one thing. Molly will not stand for it, either. Of all my girls, she's the most like me. She has no problem speaking her mind, and he'll never know what hit him."

"I knew there was something about her that I liked," Susanne said.

Both women sat back and enjoyed the scent of the roses growing nearby.

"I love roses," Susanne said. "These are extremely fragrant."

"This was a bush my father got for my mom many years ago, and each year, the smell gets stronger. And the flowers seem to last forever. My mother loved roses, too. She had such a way with them. They seemed to want to bloom for her. When she passed, I thought we'd never see roses here again, but they come up every year like she's still watching over them."

Molly and Annie remained inside. The conversation had turned silent for the rest of the meal.

The time for them to leave could not come soon enough for Carter. He simply thanked Ryan and Abby for their hospitality and got quickly into the carriage. Susanne politely invited both Ryan and Abby to New York and even gave a standing invitation to Ray Teal.

As they drove off, Abby turned to her husband.

"I hope you'll not think too badly of Brax or Susanne because of Carter."

"Of course not, Abby. I feel sorry for men like Carter. He's never satisfied with what he has, and one day, when he's passed away, someone will say he never enjoyed life, that he spent too much time striving to grab that dream."

CHAPTER ELEVEN

The sun rose to smile on the Lochlan home on the special day. Molly Lochlan was getting married. Everyone in town had shown up.

Cousin Holly, along with Mick and Mary's son and daughter, had come in from out of town. Thanks to Uncle Mick and his connections, Molly was able to get Braxton's sisters Janie and Barbara as well as their families to come to Fall River to see their little brother get married.

Upstairs in the girls' old bedroom, Meghan, Annie, and Holly were adding the final touches on Molly's gown. They added a few of Grandma Molly's beautiful yellow roses to the train of the gown.

Aunt Mary had come in just to sneak a peek and wish Molly well. Mary had been with the girls since the day they were born. She loved them as if they were her own daughters. Then Brother Daniel popped his head in to tell them Father Cahill had arrived.

"Okay, girl, it's your show now," Meghan said to Molly. "Don't forget to smile."

Just then, Ryan came into the room. When he saw his three daughters, he recalled the three young girls who used to sit on the bed to greet him on Christmas. He remembered the first time he'd put Molly on a horse and how she'd taken to it as though she'd been born on a horse.

"How do I look, Daddy?"

"Girl, you take me breath away. You look so much like your mother when she was your age. Now I have to take you downstairs and give you to another man. I'm not fond of doing that, lassie."

"I know, but I also know you want to see me happy and settled down. Besides, you're not giving me away, Daddy. I'll always be your Molly, no matter what happens."

Meghan and Annie headed out the door. Meghan stopped at the door and turned around.

"I'll see you downstairs, Molly," she said. "You look beautiful."

Molly took one last look at her room. She had so many memories there, and soon, she would be living in a new house.

"Guess we'd better start this show, right, Daddy?"

"Right, lass."

He took her arm.

"I love you, Daddy. Thank you for all this."

"And I love you, my Molly girl. It was my pleasure to do this for you."

Outside, everyone was seated, waiting for the bride. All eyes turned to the door as Molly appeared on her father's arm. Slowly, she made her way toward Braxton, who hadn't taken his eyes off her.

Father Cahill began the vows. Molly repeated after him, and Braxton was next.

Father Cahill turned to the congregation.

"Insomuch as Molly and Braxton have pledged themselves before God and all here, I now pronounce them husband and wife. Braxton, you may kiss the bride."

Braxton kissed Molly for the first time as his wife, and the crowd cheered.

The reception was held outside on the newly installed wooden dance floor. Molly had her first dance with her father while Braxton danced with his mother.

"Are you pleased, Mother?" Braxton asked.

"To see you this happy and to have all your sisters here after all these years... to see my grandchildren... I don't know what else to say." Susanne teared up. "That girl you just married is unbelievable. Don't ever lose her. She's a gem."

He looked across the dance floor and caught his wife's eye.

"Oh, you can be sure, Mother. I'll never lose her. Never."

Molly smiled as she and her father passed Braxton and his mother on the dance floor.

"Braxton is so happy, Daddy. I can't thank Uncle Mick for getting his sisters here for the wedding."

"Well, your Uncle Mick will do anything for you girls."

Molly smiled. She had done it for both Braxton and his mother.

"Did you know she has never seen her grandchildren? After all these years, this is the first time Susanne has seen them. I just can't believe how Brax's father could be so cruel."

Ryan could tell Molly was getting angry. "Girl, not today. This is your day, honey. Don't take it from you and Braxton."

"You're right, Daddy."

Mick made his way to the dance floor to take away the bride. "Happy, Molly girl?"

"Yes, Uncle Mick. Thank you for your help in getting Brax's sisters."

"My pleasure, beautiful, and may I say you look beautiful today. You know I would do anything for my nieces."

"I know, and I speak for the three of us when I say we love you so much."

"And I love you all, too, darlin'."

Mick felt a tap on his shoulder. Carter wanted to dance with his daughter-in-law. Mick graciously gave Carter Molly's hand.

"Molly, dear, you look lovely."

"Thank you, Mr. Calhan."

"Why so formal? After all, we are family now."

"All right, Dad."

"See? That wasn't so hard. I have taken the liberty of purchasing for you and Braxton a lovely home in Boston. I feel it will be an excellent first home for you two. It's in the right part of town, and a lot of the families in the neighborhood would be excellent to further Braxton's career."

Molly took a breath. "Let me get this straight, Mr. Calhan—you purchased a home for us? With all due respect, we are capable of getting our own home. We had planned to look for a small place when we got back from Virginia."

"Of course you can. You can purchase your next home, but for now, I want everything ready for you when you come back from your honeymoon. Oh, that reminds me—I'll have my secretary set up a luncheon where you will be hosting the women of the neighborhood and becoming part of their inner circle. It's important that you get off on the right foot in the community. Make sure you become a part of the various women's groups in the city. It will open doors for Braxton. I don't need to express how important a wife is to her husband's career. You'll get the hang of it after the first two or three luncheons."

Molly stopped dancing and looked at him. Suddenly, the music stopped, as well.

"No, no, I mean *no*. I'm sorry, Mr. Calhan, but I will not allow you to run my life as if I'm some child. I cannot be bought or sold or molded into the wife that you feel will make your firm more appealing to the people of Boston. I married Braxton, not the firm. I will not follow your orders as though you're the second coming of the Messiah. If you can't accept that, we don't need your house or your law office. I'm sorry for you, and we will do it on our own—with or without your approval."

Dead silence surrounded them as Molly rushed back to the house, followed by Abby, Braxton's sisters, her sisters, Mary, and Holly.

Carter, alone on the dance floor, looked around at the guests, who averted their gazes when he looked their way.

"She's a new bride," he said. "Give her a few weeks. She'll calm down and start to see things the firm's way. Seems she's a bit high strung. Must be the Irish side of her family. They tend to be a bit high strung."

He looked around for someone to agree with him, but the guests had begun sitting down at the tables.

"Now you all know she's young and inexperienced in the ways of business. She'll understand once she sees what her place is and what is expected of her. She's..."

At this point, Mick stopped Ryan from getting to Carter by pushing him back. Mick stepped on the dance floor behind Carter. He tapped Carter on the shoulder.

"Mr. Dawson," Carter said, "I'm sure you agree with me about this, don't you?"

Mick looks straight at him. "No, I don't, Mr. Calhan, and I don't appreciate you talking about my niece like that. She's not high strung, and it's not an Irish trait. It sounded to me like you were simply insulting all Irish. You see, I've known her since the day she and her sisters were born, and her folks have always taught her to be respectful to people even when they're ignorant. It's something we Irish teach our children—respect."

"Are you saying—"

"Yes, I am, Mr. Calhan. Now I feel sorry for your son and your lovely wife, 'cause somehow they have found a way to live with your ignorance, but my niece won't. You have managed to make this most important day of her life a disaster. I find that totally uncalled for and selfish on your part. Now, I'd appreciate it if you would just leave this party and head back to New York and let us enjoy this day. I can safely say that no one wants you around here anymore."

"How dare you talk to me like that!"

"Don't make me do something I'll regret, Mr. Calhan! And you are very close to forcing me to do it."

Mick turned to leave, and Carter grabbed his shoulder. That was his first mistake. Mick turned around, and his fist met Carter's jaw with enough force to send the older man across the dance floor, landing him in a row of chairs. The guests applauded, and once again, the music started up.

"Sorry, but he had it coming," Mick told Ryan.

"Don't apologize to me." Ryan chuckled. "I rather enjoyed it. I would have liked to see you give him another one for me."

Mary came rushing to Mick. If looks could kill, Mick would have been dead.

"Do you realize what you have done, Michael Dawson?"

Mick smiled sheepishly. "Yes, my dear Mary, I put an ignorant jerk in his place for disrupting my Molly's wedding."

Mary shook her head. "I don't know what I'm going to do with you. Starting a brawl with your new nephew's father."

"Ah, Mary, he had it coming. He made fun of the Irish. I don't know what you are gonna do to me, but just love me for all my days."

She put her arms around his neck. "You have that from me always. Looks like you're our knight in shining armor."

"Oh, don't give me that title. That's Ryan's job."

CHAPTER TWELVE

Despite the mess at the wedding, Braxton and Molly did come back after their honeymoon and settle in Boston. They refused Carter's home and found a lovely little house on the outskirts of town. It was a perfect first house, and Molly set about furnishing it. The first floor had the kitchen, living room, dining room, and a small study. A housekeeper's suite was upstairs, along with the three bedrooms.

Braxton proved he was a fine lawyer. Even after Molly made a scene at her wedding, the law office did do extremely well.

Molly was truly Abby's daughter. Her charm and grace made everyone who met her feel as though they had known her all their lives.

The young couple was invited to all the social functions and gala events. She was a natural in her new role as Braxton's wife, and she knew how to use her talents wisely.

Molly opened the doors of their home on Thanksgiving and Christmas for the orphans. She made sure every child in the orphanage had at least one present under the giant tree there. Many of Braxton's clients were not the wealthy people of Boston, but the poor, who had been unable to afford legal help before Braxton came. Many had to face jail time and had left their families to become wards of the state. Though Braxton's new career focus caused a rift between him and his father, Brax had become a lawyer to help all people, and not just the wealthy ones.

Almost a year passed before Molly got a letter from her cousin Holly, who was engaged and would be married in the fall. Holly's fiancé was a gentleman who worked with Holly's father. Holly had written to ask Molly to be part of her wedding party. She would have Molly and Meghan in the wedding and their husbands as their partners. She had already asked Abby if the wedding could be at the farm, and of course, Abby had said yes.

One by one, all the girls who had grown up together were getting married. All the paths they had chosen had led them back to the farm where it all started.

As the day of Holly's wedding grew closer, the girls slowly made their way back home, and the house was soon filled with the sounds of laughter and singing again.

Within a day, time seemed to turn back to the early years when the four little girls had shared the same big bedroom on the second floor of the farmhouse.

Each of them felt as if they'd never left. They enjoyed hours of spending time in the large bedroom, remembering those times so long ago. Holly had brought the gowns with her from DC so that Annie could do the alterations if there were any to be done.

Holly's younger sister Maryanne was also in the wedding party. The happiness in the young girl's eyes made the older ones even more excited.

Holly's engagement announcement read:

Miss Holly Dawson and Mr. Jesse Holmes have announced their engagement. Miss Dawson is the daughter of Mr. Michael Dawson and Mrs. Mary McVinney Dawson of Fall River, Massachusetts, and recently Washington, DC. Mr. Holmes is the son of Col. (ret.) Oliver and Mrs. Natalie Holmes of Washington, DC. Mr. Holmes resides in Washington and is employed with the state department.

After a hectic afternoon in town with the girls, Molly got out of the wagon and fainted on the ground. The girls cried for help, and Ryan came out of the house along with Daniel.

"Get the doctor then head down to the dock," Ryan told Daniel. "Brax is coming in by boat."

He took Molly in his arms and carried her to a bedroom. Annie applied cool compresses to Molly's forehead.

When Molly came to, she saw everyone around her. Brax was sitting beside her, holding her hand.

"What?" Molly croaked. "Did I miss something?"

"Well, you got off the carriage and fainted," Brax said.

"Oh. Nothing to worry about. I've done it before. Seems when I get up too fast, I faint. It's got something to do with being pregnant."

Her husband looked at her in shock. "You're pregnant? And you didn't tell me?"

"Really, Brax, it's no earth-shattering revelation. Women all over the world get pregnant."

"Maybe so, but I'm not married to all of them. I'm married to only you!"

Ryan looked at Abby and smiled. "She's definitely your daughter."

Under Braxton's eye, Molly had to stay in bed until the day of Holly's wedding. Under no circumstance did he allow her to get up.

"Really, this is a bit much. I can walk, Brax."

"You fainted," Brax said. "For all I know, you could have been doing this for a while. I will not take a chance on you hurting yourself or the baby."

The doctor had confirmed that Molly was indeed having a child. "I want to you to get some rest. You want to be at your cousin's wedding, right? So I suggest you listen to my words."

"Yes, doctor."

After he left, Molly turned back to Brax. "I swear, you all act like I can't even move an inch. Babies are born every day."

"Nonetheless, Molly, you will listen and stay in bed. I don't want anything to happen to you and the baby."

"Brax?" Molly moaned.

"You're not going to win on this. Listen to the good doctor."

CHAPTER THIRTEEN

Holly's day arrived, bright and sunny, just as it had been for all the weddings at the Lochlan farm. No matter what time of year, any function at the farm was graced with sunlight. Abby always said it was the luck of the Irish.

She had just finished icing the wedding cake when Mick and Ryan walked into the kitchen. Ryan stopped before the cake and scooped up a bit of the icing with his finger. Abby caught him and slapped his hand.

"Ryan!"

"What?"

"What are you doing? That's Holly's wedding cake!"

"It's only a little bit. You can fix it. By the way, it tastes great." He went in for another taste.

Mick hovered, waiting for his turn.

Abby stepped in. "Both of you, out of this kitchen, and don't go near this cake again."

"But, Abby, we came for some breakfast."

"In the dining room. Not in here." She noticed him looking at the ham, already sliced. "Don't even think it, Lochlan. Mick, you keep on moving, too."

Ryan protested, "Honest, Abby, I just came in for a—"

She gently pushed them toward the door. "Yes, yes, coffee is in the dining room. Annie can get you anything else. And don't you have to be somewhere? I suggest you two check on the groom. He may want to back out of this wedding if it doesn't happen soon. And stay away from this cake!"

Soon, Father Cahill came to the house. Abby and Mary followed Annie to the father, who was with a young man.

"Abby, it's so good to see you." Father Cahill greeted her with a smile.

"Always a pleasure to see you, Father," Abby said.

"I hope you don't mind," Father Cahill said, "but I took the liberty of bringing my nephew, Jack, along. He is here on a visit from Cambridge. He's a graduate from Harvard."

Abby smiled at the young man. "Welcome, Jack. This is my sister, Mary, mother of the bride, and my daughter Annie, who will be happy to help you with anything you need."

"Thank you," Jack said graciously.

"Is it true Molly is with child?" the father asked.

"Yes, she's upstairs," Abby said. "Dr. Bailey told her she has to stay in bed and rest."

"I do hope she'll be at the wedding."

"Oh, she'll be here, Father. Not even an army of angels will stop her."

Soon, the guests started to arrive, and the house was filled inside and out with people. Some of the guests were Mick's staff from DC, and he and Mary greeted them.

The ceremony was to be held in the rose garden, for it was filled with rose bushes in honor of Abby and Mary's mother. Jesse Holmes's parents, who had come to town early that morning, were sitting with Ryan and Abby.

The music began. Looking mature and elegant far beyond her fifteen years, Maryanne

Dawson appeared at the doorway of the house and slowly made her way down the aisle, followed by Meghan Bradford. Molly came after. She felt a dizzy spell coming on, but she would not let it spoil Holly's wedding.

The music changed to the bridal march, and everyone rose and looked toward the doorway, where Holly stood with her father. She started to walk down the aisle toward Jesse. Abby sat with Ryan, watching the little girl who had lived with them while she was growing up. Holly had become a woman ready to take on a new role as a wife.

Abby shed a few tears as Holly walked by. She looked so much like Abby's late sister, Jenny, it was as though Jenny were with them.

As the couple spoke their vows, Molly felt the twinge of nausea attack her again. She looked over at Brax and started to faint. Brax reached for her then carried her into the house, where he put her in the bed and stayed with her.

"I wish I could dance out there," Molly said in bed.

"Hush," Brax said. "Let's focus on getting you better."

The reception was more than even Abby had expected. Mick had arranged for everything to be brought in by train from Boston, so she and the family hadn't needed to do much. Holly danced with her father first. The guests could see the proud gleam in Mick's eye. As she and her father passed by Abby and Ryan, Holly stopped and took Ryan's arm.

"Come on, Uncle Ryan; the three of us are going to dance."

They formed a circle. As strange as it was, they were dancing and enjoying themselves. Only after the guests all left did Mick, Mary, Abby, and Ryan relax. They sat in the rose garden, listening to the sounds of the night.

Abby looked up at the moon, and Ryan followed her gaze.

"Looking for your gypsy moon, Abby?"

"No. I was just thinking how lonely it will be when everyone leaves tomorrow."

He put his arms around her. "We always have each other."

She smiled. "I know."

CHAPTER FOURTEEN

The first snow of the season had begun earlier than usual in Boston. Molly was sitting in her living room, watching the snow fall and waiting for Brax to come home from work. Since Molly's due date was soon, Brax had taken on lighter caseloads so he could be around when Molly needed him.

As the snow continued to fall, Molly noticed the streets were completely covered. Her rose bushes, which she loved, were completely white. They reminded her so much of home. Braxton had sent to England for them.

Suddenly, she felt a sharp pain. She tried to get up but fell back on the sofa. She tried again and fell back again. Just then, her housekeeper, Greta, came in and saw what was happening.

"Miss Molly, oh my, we've got to get Mr. Brax."

Greta rushed to the hall and picked up the phone. "Operator, this is Greta Seacrest. I need to reach Mr. Braxton Calhan. It's an emergency."

From the living room, Greta heard Molly crying out in pain.

"What's going on?" Braxton's voice came on the line.

"Mr. Calhan," Greta said. "Come quickly. Miss Molly is having her baby."

She hung up and rushed back to Molly, who was trying to fight back the pain.

"Mr. Braxton will be coming soon. Hang on, Miss Molly."

Each minute felt like hours to Molly. The pains came faster and sharper. She finally heard a carriage arrive. She prayed it was Brax. The front door flew open, and Brax rushed to Molly's side.

"I already called the midwife from the office," he said.

She moved and screamed out in pain. "Tell the midwife to hurry."

"She's coming," Braxton said. "Greta, get me a blanket. Hurry."

That night, in the worst snowstorm of the season, Sarah Elizabeth Calhan came into the world, weighing nine pounds and ten ounces. She was the beautiful new addition to a family that would show her how to love and give kindness and compassion to others. She had so many great role models to look to down the road.

Braxton had been waiting for three hours to see his wife and child. So many thoughts about their health and well-being raced through his mind. When he was told he could go in, he raced into the hospital room.

Molly looked up from the bed and smiled when she saw Braxton looking at her and baby Sarah. He kissed Molly on the forehead then Sarah.

"She's beautiful," he told Molly. "She looks like your mother."

"Will you send a wire to Mom and Dad?" Molly asked. "I want them to know everything is all right."

"I'll send it in the morning."

"Don't forget."

"I won't." He kissed her on the head. "I love you, Molly Calhan."

She nodded weakly. She was getting sleepy.

The next morning, Brax kept his promise and sent a wire to the Lochlans, as well as one to his parents. Due to the weather, Abby and Ryan had to wait to travel to Boston. Abby was heartbroken. She wanted to be there with Molly, but Ryan had promised he would get her there as soon as the tracks were passable.

Brax didn't receive a response from his parents, but he hadn't expected one. Carter Calhan had not seen or spoken to Molly since their wedding day, and she had only been to their home once.

Three days later, when the tracks were clear, Ryan and Abby took the train to Boston to see their granddaughter. The little girl was extremely fussy until her grandmother arrived. No one had been able to stop her from crying until the moment Abby took her in her arms. The baby became quiet and even smiled at her.

The baby seemed to know that Abby was her grandmother, and she was content to stay in her arms all the time.

Abby nicknamed her Sassy. And Sassy she became for the rest of her life. Four years later, Bryan Michael joined the family, named after the three men in Molly's life, Brax, Ryan, and Mick.

Things were going very well for Braxton, and he had built a solid reputation in Boston as a fair and honest lawyer. That was why the town leaders were considering him for the city's next judge.

The wonderful opportunity would lead to other political fields, but Braxton first wanted to discuss it with Molly. He would have to consider numerous things before giving an answer. With the city leaders waiting for his answer, Braxton received a telegram that changed his life.

The wire was from New York and simply read:

Mr. Braxton Calhan. Boston, Mass.

Mr. Calhan, it is with deep regret that I am to tell you that your father passed away last evening. Your presence is required here in New York as soon as possible.

John Singleton esq

Braxton placed the telegram on his desk and just sat there for a few moments. All these years, the man had seemed invincible, almost immortal, but he was gone.

Over the next hour, Brax changed his case schedule so he could leave for New York as soon as possible. When he arrived home, Molly greeted him at the door. He'd had his secretary call her and tell her what had happened.

She gave him a big hug. "I'm so sorry, Brax."

He held her close for a few moments before walking into the living room.

"Got the wire at the office. My father's lawyer, John Singleton, expressed I should be in New York as soon as possible. I think he wants to have the will read immediately after the funeral. I thought I'd leave today and be back in three days."

"Don't be silly, Brax. We'll all go to New York. I can't be leaving your mother alone at a time like this."

"Molly, what about—"

"There's nothing here that can't wait, Brax. The garden club can manage without me for one meeting. I can take Sassy and Bryan out of school. After all, Carter was their grandfather. By the way, has anyone notified your sisters of his passing?"

"Do you think they would come?"

"They would want to be with your mother at this time."

He looked at her. After over fifteen years of being married to her, he was still amazed by her compassion for others in their time of need. Though Molly had not spoken to Carter Calhan since her wedding day, she'd never kept her husband from seeing his father or her children from seeing their grandparents. Sometimes she met only with Susanne, and they would have lunch and discuss their lives like old friends.

The entire family was on the next train to New York. Once they got there, Brax learned what Carter Calhan had in mind for him—Braxton was faced with a decision that would be a turning point in his life.

Carter Calhan's will expressly stated that his wife was to receive his entire estate. The law firm, in which he was senior partner, was to be given to his only son, Braxton. Upon hearing this, Brax was stunned. He approached John Singleton.

"I have a practice in Boston, Mr. Singleton. I have no interest in leaving my home and practice. I'm sure any one of my father's partners is capable of taking over the firm and continuing its success. There is no need for me to come into the firm."

John Singleton looked up from his desk. "I'm sorry, Braxton, but the practice you have in Boston was funded by the firm here in New York. The New York firm holds the title on the mortgage, and he had arranged for the Boston firm to be sold whether or not you take the position here in New York. I have his expressed orders that you return back to New York and take over the firm or go out on your own. Mind you, these are his words, not mine."

Braxton knew very well that it was all his father's doing. Even in death, Carter Calhan still wanted to rule over his family. He had made no provisions for his two daughters in the will. They had crossed him, and Carter felt they no longer existed.

Braxton looked at the partners in his father's firm; many of them had been with the firm since before Braxton was even born. He had learned so much from each of them.

"Gentlemen, I just want to say I have no intention of taking my father's place in the firm. I plan to attend his service and head back to Boston to my practice there. I trust you all can come to some compromise on how the firm will continue in his absence."

"Braxton, the office will be sold within three days' time."

"Then, gentlemen, I quit the firm," Braxton said boldly. "I will start my own firm in Boston and will not have any ties with this firm. I will be on the next train back to Boston after the service tomorrow afternoon."

Eli Stamford, one of the firm's oldest lawyers, spoke up. "You can't be serious. To give up all this?"

Braxton turned to look at the man who had encouraged him to go into law to begin with.

"Oh, but I do mean it, Eli. What am I leaving? Don't you understand? In New York, I'll always be Carter Calhan's son. Always in his shadow. Well, this time, I want to be Braxton Calhan esquire, my own man, not someone's son. You know, my wife was right when she told me how to deal with my father on our wedding day. She said there were two ways to deal with Carter—either give in to his way or get out before he destroys you. Well, I'm leaving before he can destroy me." He turned again and walked out of the conference room.

Mr. Singleton called out after him as he left. "Mr. Calhan, I insist your things be removed from the building in three days."

"The building will be empty by tomorrow, Mr. Singleton."

He didn't look back. He headed straight to the hotel where Molly and the kids were. When he walked in the door, Molly knew by the look on his face that she didn't need to ask how things went.

"We're leaving tomorrow, right after the service."

"But, but what about your mother, Brax? You can't just walk off on her."

"I don't want to discuss this. We leave tomorrow."

She turned and walked over to the window. "We'll be ready tomorrow, not to worry."

He went over to her and put his arms around her. "I'm sorry, Molly. I had no right to lash out at you."

"Did Carter back you into a corner again?"

"Even in death, he manages to get to me. But it's not going to happen anymore. I've finally taken a stand against him."

She turned around and looked deep into his eyes. "What happened?"

"He left me the senior partnership in the firm and wanted me to move back here. Here, I would be Carter's boy, not Mr. Calhan. I don't want that, nor do I want to leave all our plans and dreams in Boston and just to forget about them. We've worked too hard to build a life there, and I'm not letting them go just because Carter Calhan says so."

"And if you don't?"

"Well, he's selling the office in three days either way."

"Brax, why is he doing this?"

"Because he's Carter Calhan."

"He would destroy you and his grandchildren just because he was mad?"

"He can't win. I quit today. I've decided to take the job as judge back home. I will not leave Boston. It's our home, and our children were born there."

"I admire you." Molly kissed him on the cheek. For him to start out at the bottom all over again was so brave. She had spoken many times, saying that they could always use her money, but he'd always declined. She knew he would show them all that he was his own man. But he really needed her help.

"Braxton, we can use my money now, just until you get your new office set up. You can pay it back. For years, you have been supporting us. Let me just this once."

He looked at her. "Just to get us on our feet?"

"That's all. A one-time thing."

"I can pay you back?"

"Yes, dear."

He put his arms around her. "Okay, you win."

CHAPTER FIFTEEN

Braxton did become a judge. There was even talk of him running for attorney general, but he felt one politician in the family was enough, and Meghan's husband, Adam, had that all sewn up.

Brax wanted to start on another path. He applied for a teaching position at Emerson College, and Braxton became the new law professor. Emerson was a fine college, and teaching meant he could help budding young lawyers by giving them his years of experience in the courts. He also helped his colleagues in the profession when he sent letters of recommendations out for his brightest students.

Though Braxton no longer had an office, he was never too busy to help out a friend in need, and he would often sit at the kitchen table with a client. He had proved to himself that he didn't need Carter's backing to be successful. He had Molly as his lucky charm.

With the children grown and soon be off to college, Molly and Brax were thinking of a smaller house, maybe something more toward the country. He knew how she loved the country and how much she missed being around animals all the time. He even considered getting a place where she could have a stable.

The Lochlans still met for the holidays at Fall River, but the farm held bittersweet memories. Ryan had passed on four years ago.

There was such loneliness in Abby, a need to hear Ryan's voice and feel his touch. She would sit in the rose garden for hours, just remembering the man she loved with her whole heart and soul, the man who'd followed his dream to America and made her part of that dream.

Molly missed the farm. She hadn't been there since Ryan's service. She found it hard to believe that her father was gone, and even harder to see how sad her mother was without him. From the first day of their marriage, Ryan had been her rock.

Annie was the one who had found her mother on the living room floor, cradling Ryan's head. It had been a typical day on the farm, and after dinner, when he went into the living room to sit beside Abby, he stumbled and fell.

He had looked up at Abby and smiled. "I'm sorry, Abby." He'd tried to get up but couldn't move.

"Ryan! Ryan, what's wrong?"

"Abby, you'll have to follow this dream alone. But don't worry, darlin', I'll be waiting for you on the other side. I'll never leave you, ever. I love you, my sweet Abby."

With that, he passed from one world into the next. Abby held his lifeless body for what seemed like forever. She felt as if she were holding a sleeping baby.

That was how Annie found her, tears streaming down her cheeks, but not making a sound.

Annie had tried to get her mother to get off the floor. "Mama, I need you to get up and onto the sofa."

"I can't leave him, Annie. He needs me. Look, he's sleeping."

Annie knew she had to get someone else to help get her father into another room.

She looked out the back window and saw Ryan's horse was still saddled. If she could get to her brother Daniel, who was not far, he could help her. She had to act quickly. There wasn't any time to waste.

She headed out the back door, mounted her father's horse, and rode out.

Soon, Daniel and Annie raced back to the house. Abby was still sitting on the floor, holding Ryan. Daniel looked at his mother in pity. She had always been able to handle any crisis. Seeing her this way was a shock. He walked over to her and gently lifted her from the floor.

"Mama, I'm going to have to move Papa. I need you to move to the sofa."

In a small voice, Abby said, "You will be gentle with him, Daniel. Promise. Don't hurt him."

"I know, Mama. I promise I won't hurt him."

Gently, Daniel lifted his father and carried him into the bedroom. When he came back to the living room, he sat down on the sofa near his mother.

"What happened, Mama?"

Abby had such sadness in her eyes. "He was smiling and happy, like he always was, and suddenly, he fell. I thought he tripped, but he just couldn't get up. It was as though he couldn't move his legs. He kept saying he was sorry and something about a dream he followed... something about a dream... and then he smiled at me, and he was gone."

Annie looked up at Daniel, and they both knew there was no way Abby was making any sense. She was going into shock and she needed a doctor.

"I'm going into town to fetch the doctor," Daniel said. "I want you to stay with Annie till I get back."

"All right, Danny. But there is no need to worry. I'll stay here until your father gets back. I promise."

Daniel turned to Annie and whispered, "Watch her."

While in town, Daniel sent wires to Meghan, Molly, and of course, Uncle Mick.

Later, the doctor gave Abby something so she could sleep. He suggested she should get some rest and he would be back in the morning to see her.

He had made arrangements for Ray Teal to bring a carriage to transport the body to Conrad's Funeral Parlor in town. Mr. Conrad had been a friend of the family for years.

He had done the funerals for Abby's father and Jenny, as well as Abby's uncle Gideon. As the day grew into evening and then night, friends stopped by the house to offer their sympathies to the family.

Molly and Brax were the first to arrive. When Molly entered the house, she felt the whole house sobbing at the loss of the head of their family.

The children took up the task of planning the funeral since Abby was in no shape to do it. Meghan and Adam had sent a wire that they were on their way and would arrive the next day.

Slowly, the house filled with family. Everyone walked about, still knowing the loss they would all feel in the coming days.

In the late evening, the family heard the sound of a carriage making its way to the front of the house. Molly and Brax were sitting with Annie in the living room.

"Who could that be at this hour?" Brax asked.

Brax headed for the door then waited for the knock. He opened the door to find Mick and Mary standing there.

"Uncle Mick, Aunt Mary, what are you doing at this hour of the night?"

"We've come to be with Abby. We took the last train to Boston and rented a carriage to get down here."

"Aunt Mary," Brax said, "you look exhausted. Come sit down."

Brax led her into the living room, where Molly and Annie were. They got up to hug their aunt, who, in fact, was feeling horribly tired from the journey.

"How is Abby taking it?" Mick asked.

"Not good," Molly said. "She seems to think Daddy's going to walk through the door."

Mary shook her head and began to cry. Mick put his arm around her.

"Mary, we agreed we wouldn't cry. Abby needs someone to be strong for her."

"I know, but she's been through so much. First Mama and Annie, then Jennie and Papa and Uncle Gideon. How much more can this woman take?"

She broke down, and so did Molly.

"Come on, girls," Mick said. "I know it's hard, but let's remember we need to be strong for Abby."

They all knew he was right and brushed away their tears.

CHAPTER SIXTEEN

When all the family was in Fall River, they had a viewing and a service at the funeral home the next day. The burial was a private matter, and only Father Cahill, who was invited to bless the soul, and of course Ray Teal, who supplied carriages for the family members, were invited.

At the request of the children, Mick said a few words about his dear friend.

"Ryan came here to America after the potato famine. He knew there was nothing left for him in Ireland, and he believed that his dream was in America. As fate would have it, we were put together in the railroad and become fast friends. We were sent down from Boston to Fall River to help with the railroad.

"His love story started when he was sent out to talk to a Mr. Daniel McVinny. Well, as you all know, Mr. McVinny had lovely daughters, Abby, Jenny, Mary, and little Annie. Ryan seemed to be spending a lot of time at the farm, and one day, I followed him. The look on his face when Abby walked out the door was priceless. I knew she was it for him. He was hooked. Well, seemed ol' Dan liked him, and even trusted him, and through Ryan, the railroad got Daniel's permission to use the road to take supplies to us at Fall River.

"I don't have to tell you how things turned out. Ryan got his fair young maiden, and thanks to Ryan, I married my wife. Both of them from the family. I was there when his children were born. He even gave one of his boys Michael as a middle name. I was there when Molly and Annie were killed. It was one of the saddest days we ever faced together. And I was there when Daniel died. Now I'm here doing the hardest thing I have ever had to do: say goodbye to my best friend.

"Fate put us together, just a pair of young lads with dreams of finding that pot o' gold. The proudest day of Ryan's life besides his wedding was when his girls were born. Girls, I was there when you were born, and I tell you I love you as if you were me own."

The girls had tears rolling down their cheeks.

"Danny and Tom, you both turned into fine young men, and you made your dad proud of you always. He will always be looking down on you to guide you. I'd like to end this with a short story. T'was a young man from the land of the wee folk and dreams, who came to these shores to follow a dream—one that promised a better life—and no longer would he roam. That place offered him peace, happiness, and a home of his own. He loved his dear Abby for all of his days, and he's still here with us. We can feel him in so many ways. And so we place him to rest and we pray he sleeps peacefully, and when our time comes, we hope he'll be waiting to greet us."

He leaned down and placed a rose on top of Ryan's coffin. "Until we meet again, Ryan."

He helped Abby walk over to the coffin. Mary held her on her other side.

Though the service was private, it felt as if the whole town had come. Everyone had been close to the family for years. The room was packed full.

Abby looked around, thinking she was just having a bad dream or that she was at someone else's funeral. She kept hoping to see Ryan come through that front door to greet her.

She eventually realized Ryan was never going to come through those doors again. She would never hold him or feel his kiss on her cheek. Yet there was one thing that not even death could take from her. She would always have the memory of his touch, his spirit, and his soul. Each room in their house had a special memory of Ryan and how much he'd loved it.

He'd once been a young man who'd come into her life quite by accident, and yet her whole family had fallen in love with him. The day they got married was like a dream.

After a while, Abby bounced back and returned to being the same Abby everyone knew. She smiled more and took an active interest in the people around her again. Her children, especially Annie, were relieved.

Annie was the last of the triplets to wed. With her sisters and cousin Holly all married, it was now her time.

Once again, the Lochlan farm was in wedding mode, and all the girls were back home again. Everyone was there: Meghan and Adam, with their three children; Molly and Brax, with their two children; Holly and Jesse, with their five children; and course Uncle Mick, Aunt Mary, Maryann, and her husband, Peter.

Abby was so glad to see that Annie had found someone. Of all her girls, Annie was the gentlest, with so much love to give. Abby didn't want her to be alone like she was. Annie should have a man who loved her and children. Oh yes, she should have children; she was so wonderful with them.

On Annie's big day, her sisters fussed over her the way she had fussed over them. Like the other girls, Annie took that walk down the aisle of the rose garden. Uncle Mick took her in his arms. She looked so beautiful in a simple white dress and short veil.

Abby smiled with tears in her eyes as she watched her Annie become a newlywed. The young and happy couple would live on the farm and carry on the tradition that Abby's father had started so long ago.

Abby felt a gentle breeze and could've sworn she heard a soft voice whisper, "She looks beautiful. We're here with all of you, watching her."

She looked around, and everyone was watching the bride and groom. Mary looked at Abby and nodded. Mary had heard it, too—the voice of their mother.

Their parents and Ryan were there with them.

CHAPTER SEVENTEEN

A year passed. The house was busy and filled with the laughter of family members. So many years had passed since there was a newborn in the family. Everyone was happy that it was now Annie's turn. Her sisters had gathered at Fall River for the event, and even Aunt Mary and Uncle Mick were there from Washington. Soft-spoken Annie was finally going to be a mama and bring new life into the home.

Mary was busy in the kitchen, making coffee, as the family waited in the hallway, waiting for the doctor to come out and give everyone the good news.

Molly and Meghan were in the room with Annie to help her. With her last push, Annie gave birth to a beautiful little girl.

Abby was outside, watching a shooting star whisk across the sky. She heard a familiar voice.

"Make a wish."

She found herself answering aloud. "I wish you were still here, Ryan."

"I am, Abby girl."

She looked up and saw Ryan standing in front of her, smiling and offering his hand.

"Come on, Abby, let's look at the moonlight."

"You can't be here. I mean, you're...."

Suddenly, Mick came out and found her in the garden on a bench asleep.

"Abby, Abby, wake up."

"No," she muttered. "Ryan, I don't want you to go. Ryan..." She opened her eyes and saw Mick.

"What are you doing here?" she blurted out.

He only smiled gently at her.

"Well, I'm sorry I'm not Ryan, but I came out here to tell you that Annie had a girl. Now why don't you join us in the house and toast the newest lass in the Lochlan family."

He offered his hand to her, just as Ryan had in her dream. She got up and walked back into the house with him. When they entered the house, Mary gave them both a glass of champagne to toast the newborn.

Braxton took the lead. "I propose a toast to our lovely Annie, her husband, and their newborn daughter, Amy."

"Why the name Amy?" Mary asked.

Meghan smiled. "A for Abby, M for Molly, and Y because both names end in Y."

"Here's to Amy!" Molly said.

Annie was resting upstairs while everyone was celebrating, so Abby made her way up the stairs and into the bedroom. There in the bed was a tired Annie and little Amy.

"Hi, sweetheart." Abby peered down at the cute little face.

"Hi, Mama. Well, here she is. I hope you like the name."

Abby took the baby in her arms and smiled down at the precious little one. "Oh, I think the name is perfect. And she's perfect."

Later that evening, Abby sat in the rocker, holding her new granddaughter. She hummed a lullaby to little Amy as she drifted off to sleep.

Abby heard laughter coming from inside the house. The house felt full, and so did her heart. Molly, Meghan, and now Annie were all married and happy. She had a lot to be grateful for as a mother.

She looked up at the moon and saw the gypsies dancing in the moonlight. That was a story she shared with Ryan and the kids. She smiled, knowing that one day, she would tell this story to Amy. And one day, Amy would pass this same story on to her children.

About the Author

Chloe Emile writes sweet, clean romance, whether it's contemporary or historical. She can usually be found working on her next novel, eating takeout with her husband, or watching rom-coms.

www. ChloeEmile.com

Chloe Emile

www.ingramcontent.com/pod-product-compliance
Lightning Source LLC
Chambersburg PA
CBHW051956170626
46808CB00007B/2644